ALSO BY BEN DOLNICK

You Know Who You Are

Zoology

AT THE BOTTOM OF EVERYTHING

ToM

YTHING

Ben
Dolnick

PANTHEON

Library of Congress Cataloging-in-Publication Data
Dolnick, Ben.
At the bottom of everything / Ben Dolnick.
p. cm.
ISBN 978-0-307-90798-1
1. Boys—Fiction. 2. Male friendship—Fiction.
3. Forgiveness—Fiction. I. Title.
PS3604.O44A83 2013
813'.6—dc23
2012042259

www.pantheonbooks.com

Jacket design by Pablo Delcan
Book design by Claudia Martinez

Printed in the United States of America
First Edition
2 4 6 8 9 7 5 3 1

For my grandmother

and

for Elyse

Here is the real core of the religious problem:
Help! help!

—WILLIAM JAMES

· *One* ·

———————————

I've noticed that whenever I tell the story of going to look for Thomas (all it takes is a couple of beers, like quarters into a jukebox), at some point whoever I'm talking to will say two things:

(1) You're such a good friend!

and

(2) How could you just pick up and leave like that?

I was nothing like a good friend, and I could only pick up and leave like that because the thing I was picking up and leaving was no longer, in any recognizable sense, a life. But I don't say this. My conversation self, the one I send out to bars and parties and weddings, is a half-truth-spouting machine. Here I'll try to do better.

I'd spent the last couple of years (really the years since I was fifteen) ignoring the fact that Thomas needed me, as if his life were a flashing Check Engine light in the corner of my dashboard. I'd let emails from his mom pile up so long that it would have been worse, I convinced myself, to respond that late than just not to respond at all. I'd become an expert at changing the subject whenever his name came up (*did you ever think he'd drop out of school? did you hear he was in the hospital? what's he doing in India?*). I'd even, one especially unproud morning, turned and speed-walked out of Safeway because I'd seen Thomas's dad, or someone who looked like Thomas's dad, rooting around in the bin of red peppers.

But of course shame was going to catch up with me sooner or later. Shame or Thomas's mom, who startled me outside the CVS on Wisconsin Avenue one day when I'd just bought a box of condoms.

"You're just hell to get ahold of," she said, smiling. I held my bag behind my back. "Do you have time to come back to our place? Richard would love to see you."

"Oh," I said, "I'm actually . . ." and pointed off vaguely behind me.

She nodded. "You know Thomas talks about you as much as anybody," she said. My heart was racing, reasonably enough. "I know he'd love to hear from you."

"I'll write to him," I said, and I did my best to sound as if the thing that had been stopping me until then was just that it had never occurred to me.

We hugged (this took some ginger CVS-bag maneuvering on my part) and promised to see each other soon. "Send your mother our love," she called out as she got into her car (a new Volvo, this one blue). I was fake smiling and murmuring for a block and a half.

Thomas had been the smartest kid at Dupont Prep, the last person anyone would have pegged for disaster. And I, semi-reasonable soccer player and wearer of striped polo shirts, had been his best friend. We were, for a few years, one of those pairs, like Arthur Miller and Marilyn Monroe, that no one could quite believe in or understand.

Anyway, childhood friends, given a decade or two, turn into strangers. Their parents don't. I could more or less convince myself that the Thomas I'd been doing my best not to think about was someone else entirely, but his mom (who looked so pale and defeated, who was probably even then asking Richard to guess who she'd run into) was unmistakably the same woman who'd driven me home when I'd forgotten my retainer, who'd bought me calamine lotion when I came back from field day with poison ivy. But I didn't turn around.

I won't try to defend myself except to say that my own life still seemed to me complicated and demanding enough that I didn't think I had room in it for Thomas. And that I turned out to be as wrong, in imagining the course of those next few months, as I'd ever been about anything.

But just then I only knew that I'd barely escaped a visit to the Pells, and that Anna was waiting for me. I hurried back to my car like a fish released, just in time, from a barbed and rusting hook.

———

When all this happened I was twenty-six, which didn't seem to me at all young. I'd recently realized that I couldn't say anymore, when people (great-uncles, overzealous librarians) asked, that I'd "just finished college," and that no one wanted to know now what I wanted to be; they wanted to know what I did.

Which was: tutoring. "Ohhh! Tutoring! That must be so . . . [hard/interesting/wonderful]." It was hard, in the sense that all of life, particularly the bits you have to spend with sullen eleven-year-olds, is hard. And it was interesting, in that it meant I got to see a great number of strangers' kitchens and bedrooms and medicine cabinets packed with antidepressants and Vaseline. It was only wonderful at the ends of sessions, when I would nod farewell to a parent or babysitter and spill back out into the world, free and light and finished.

For the two years after college I'd had a more conventional job, at a political magazine on Capitol Hill. This magazine was tiny and well respected, perpetually on the brink of bankruptcy, overseen by its eighty-something FDR-revering founder, staffed by young and exhausted and brilliant people who moved on after a year or two and haunted you forever after with their bylines. Every issue was an emergency, and in the middle of my first real assignment, something about the transformation of the domestic auto industry, I had a panic attack (my first in years), complete with a terrifying/ mortifying ambulance ride, after which my boss made clear, if it wasn't clear already, that I was probably in the wrong line of work.

So that spring I became a tutor, which seemed, along with being a nanny, to be one of the loopholes people my age had discovered in the professional world, a way of making a reasonable amount of money without working particularly hard or doing anything more soul-crushing than absolutely necessary. My mom and stepdad were appeased by the thought that I was just biding my time before going off to law school and becoming a public defender (which I still thought I might do), and I was appeased by the thought that I got to spend all my nights with Claire.

I'd met Claire when we were undergrads, but we'd only known each other well enough to smile when we shared an elevator or when we passed each other in the library. She was one of the girls, of whom there were dozens at Penn, who I'd see and think, *In another life, maybe, yes.* Red hair, pale skin, freckles that weren't so much countable as a kind of wallpaper pattern. She was in things like improv troupes and student movies, on the fringes of the theater crowd but not quite so pretentious or pleased with herself as most of them seemed to be. She always had a boyfriend, usually another actor.

I first saw her in D.C. at a party in Adams Morgan just before I left the magazine. It's always unsettling, seeing people you've almost but not quite forgotten about—not because they've changed (she'd hardly changed at all) but because they've gone on existing, finding jobs and making friends and moving apartments, all without the help of your thinking about them. So there she was, Claire Brier, standing in front of the little table that someone had set up with bottles of vodka and juice and red plastic cups. We hugged when we saw each other, despite never having hugged when we'd seen each other regularly. We carried our drinks over to the window, because even though it was April the heat was on in the apartment, and while we talked she fanned herself with her hand. She turned out to be living alone on U Street, working at a think tank, still doing improv on the weekends. She finished her vodka and poured herself another. She looked, I thought and think, like a girl who should live on a rocky beach in New England, drink enormous mugs of dark tea, dig up clams.

"You always seemed like such a *dude*," she said after we'd been talking for a while. "I thought you were a Flip Cup kind of person."

"I thought you were a vocal exercises kind of person."

"*Mi mi mi mi mi.*"

We hugged again before she left, more confidently than before, and she told me that I should come to her next improv show.

I did, and that did it. There were, in those first weeks, afternoon coffees that ended with us on a bench near her office, her legs in my lap; there were mornings of having to unmake the bed to find our underwear; there was kissing good-bye on the Metro platform. By that first fall together we were spending almost every night at her apartment, reading next to each other in bed, having conversations between the shower and the bedroom.

"So I guess this is what it feels like," she said once, when we were leaning forehead to forehead, the only two people on the long escalator in Union Station.

I wish I could take that year, like the salvageable bits of a meal dropped on the floor, and separate it from what happened next, which now seems minor but which at the time seemed baffling and tragic and unbelievable. What happened is: she broke up with me. "You had a bad breakup," my mom said when I was over for dinner one night, in a summing-up-and-moving-on voice. (Are there good breakups? Are there break-ups that leave both people feeling that they've just emerged not from a washing machine but from a bittersweet and not-too-long movie?)

There was the philosophical version, which would settle over me sometimes as I was falling asleep—I never entirely opened up to her and this little flaw, like a crack in a glass table, had no choice but to spread—and then there was the battle-flashback version that I spent most of my days trapped in. The fight outside her building, when someone leaned out from a high window and called out, "Get a divorce!" The bleary Sunday morning in the kitchen when she said, "I don't know why we're doing this anymore." The night on the couch when we both cried while *Diners, Drive-Ins and Dives* played in the background.

In the middle of my tutoring sessions now, while the fifth grader I was supposed to be paying attention to burrowed through a sheet of word problems, I'd look up into the black living-room windows and think: *Cold and alone.* I don't know where this phrase came from, or what *cold* had to do with anything, but the words were like a lyric that had eaten into my brainstem: *cold and alone,* waiting for the light to change; *cold and alone,* eating Chex for dinner; *cold and alone,* listening to my roommate and his girlfriend have sex at half past two in the morning.

I'd gotten used to treating my apartment, in my Claire days, as not much more than a place to keep my clothes and pick up the mail, but suddenly I was spending my nights drinking beer with Joel on the futon, watching Craig Ferguson. "Are you gonna be OK?" he sometimes said.

"I don't know."

"Ah, come on, you are."

I knew Joel from college too—he'd been the guy in my freshman dorm who knew where in Philadelphia to buy good weed—but now we seemed to have not much more reason to live together than any two people standing in line together at the bank.

One night, while I was lying with my cheek pressed

against the rug between the coffee table and the TV, thinking for whole minutes about things like whether I should roll over to reach for my water glass, I called Claire twenty-three times. At first I had urgent things to say, things I was sure would change her mind, but after half a dozen calls I couldn't remember what they were, and if she'd picked up I would just have had to groan, like a cow whose legs have given out. Another night I stood outside her building saying her name, first in an embarrassed bark, then louder and louder until I was bawling on U Street, promising myself that I would never again feel anything except sympathy for the people I saw ranting in front of the White House. I was going to tell her about my childhood, tell her about Thomas, about Mira Batra; I was going to split my life open and spill it onto her front steps like a full-to-bursting bag of coffee grounds and orange rinds.

This happened to be the fall of 2008, a few weeks before the election, when everyone in D.C., and maybe everyone in the country, had been gripped by a brain fever that was making them email each other poll results and interview clips and enormous heartfelt diatribes about how normally they don't get involved in politics but now, with the stakes so high . . . For me all that was like the Traffic and Weather Together updates on AM radio. The only headlines I cared about, and I cared about them so much that I would run from the apartment door to my computer without taking my coat off, were Claire's Facebook updates, which she hadn't yet blocked me from seeing.

> So fun running into you guys last night! We should grab a drink!

> Hahaha tell B I miss her please, OK?

> Anybody else starting to crave chili? Mmmm.

Each of these, next to a stamp-sized picture of Claire smiling in the white snow hat she'd once sat holding on my bed, made me feel like one of the stockbrokers in the pictures on all the newsstands. DOW DROPS 777 POINTS, WORST SINCE DEPRESSION.

Who is B?

Where was Claire when she ran into people last night?

Doesn't that "Mmmm" sound like someone who's got a new boyfriend?

These questions gripped me for some of the least happy hours I'd spent since high school, slouching in the filth of my bedroom, clicking and clicking, unable to summon the energy even to turn on the lights. The way I remember it, I spent those months half sick, unshaven, shuffling along wind-tunnel streets with my hands buried in pocket-nests of disintegrating Kleenex. Suffering impairs judgment; there should be flashing lights, a surgeon general's warning, celebrity-sponsored ad campaigns.

I say that Thomas was the smartest boy at my new school, but I want to make clear just what I mean by that.

When I was twelve my mom remarried and we moved from Baltimore to a suburb just outside D.C., so in seventh grade I started at Dupont Prep, where everybody seemed to come with a title as much a part of them as a last name. Teddy Minor: best athlete. Jason Vorsheck: best musician. Vanessa Stoyke: best writer.

Thomas's title was the most impressive but also the hardest to pin down. Because there were definitely kids who were smarter in the sense of doing better on math tests—there were boys who were essentially human computers, humming autistically away while they filled out problem sets meant for college students. And there were kids who had a practical supercompetence that Thomas never came close to—they were on the robotics team, they fixed the A/V system, they wore T-shirts with Nietzsche quotes.

But all of those people's intelligence had something glitchy about it, something vulnerable and freakish; what set Thomas apart, I think, was that he somehow managed, in his hundred-pound body and New Balance sneakers, to give the impression of being *wise*. Teachers talked to him about things they would never have talked to the rest of us about—their sick parents, their boredom with *Jacob Have I Loved,* their hopes of writing a screenplay. If the discussion in an English class or a grade-wide meeting got especially tense or complicated, you could always count on Thomas, raising his hand so slightly that it was almost as if he were apologizing for it, to say something that would work like a sudden gush of cold water on a burn. "I wonder if Amelia's and Harold's arguments are actually variations on the same point . . ." "This may be very similar to what David was saying earlier, but if what we're really talking about is whether some people at Dupont feel excluded from the bulk of the student body, then I think . . ."

People liked him but there was something impersonal about their feelings; he was, especially as middle school went on, like the school's prize oak tree.

A lot of this had to do with dating, or "dating," since couples at Dupont didn't, in seventh grade, go on actual dates. Jenny and Stuart were a couple, so on Valentine's Day Jenny gave him a key chain with a red rubber heart. That was all. Lauren and Neil. Alex and Alex. Me and a pretty but nearly mute girl named Rebecca. It was as if there were some disaster headed our way, a tidal wave or a meteor, and we all had to pair off for the sake of the human race.

Thomas was shut out of all this, mostly because he had no female equivalent. He was too strange, too impressive, too mature; dating him would have been like dating Mr. Davis, the seventy-year-old British drama teacher.

Some of this must also have had to do with the way he looked, which wasn't bad, really, but was as much alien as boy. He was the palest person I'd ever seen, almost translucent (the one time I remember him being teased was when he took off his shirt at a pool party and revealed this nipple-less body the color of a boiled peanut). His eye sockets were enormous, delicate caves, like dented eggshells. At my old school there had been a boy with leukemia, and Thomas made something of the same impression; he'd been taken out of the oven too early, he needed another coat of skin. But with Thomas the effect wasn't so much to make him seem weak (although he was definitely weak); it was to make him seem intimidating, the way a reptile can be intimidating. Why did he look so steadily at your eyes when you talked? Didn't he ever bite his nails or tap his feet? It was impossible to picture him kissing someone (kissing was as far as any of these couples went), or even just dancing.

And he spoke, at twelve years old, so calmly, with such carefully constructed sentences, that it was hard to believe at first that he wasn't faking it. Some people thought it was a slight British accent, but it wasn't that—it was more of a cigarette-holder accent, the voice of a professor musing at the head of a seminar table. I used to do an impression of him that reliably brought tears to Matt Corrigan's eyes. "If the assignment sheet is right that you'd like us to read chapters three and four tonight (and I assume that it is), then should this chapter four over the weekend actually be a chapter five?"

But there were things he wasn't good at (mental things, I mean; at sports he was a disaster), and it was always a surprise to discover one. Spanish, for instance. I'd never taken a foreign language—they didn't start until seventh grade at my old school—but by my third week at Dupont I was speaking as well as Thomas, who'd been studying it since third grade and still couldn't roll his *r*'s. And music. When he picked up his trumpet in band he was like a newborn deer, so clumsy and feeble.

I played percussion, which meant that I stood right behind the brass section. I was in the perfect position to see that while Thomas sat there, his legs pressed together as if he had to go to the bathroom, his trumpet tilted toward the ceiling, he was faking it, straining his cheeks, bugging his eyes.

We played movie themes and marches, so loudly that you could feel the out-of-tune-ness as a buzz in your bones. Our teacher was a little gray-haired rooster of a man named Mr.

Adams. He walked around the music room holding a coffee mug with some sort of musical joke on it (NEVER B FLAT; SOMETIMES B SHARP; ALWAYS B NATURAL), looking for reasons to yell. We knew he'd found one when he set his mug down on the piano. "*You incompetent twerp! Play it! Don't come in here and insult the rest of us with this . . .* bwwap, bwwap, bwwap. *Play it like you mean it! Play it with some BALLS!*"

Since he wasn't a classroom teacher, Mr. Adams didn't know or didn't care that everyone else at Dupont revered Thomas. To him Thomas was just the sickly little seventh grader who tried to use his braces as an excuse not to play. "*Sweet Cheeks!* Everyone else shut up, I want to hear just what Sweet Cheeks is doing, I want all of you to hear it. Ready? One-and, two-and, three-and, four-and . . . *What? What's that you're saying? I can't hear you.*"

"I haven't had a chance to practice this piece, actually."

"You haven't had a chance to practice this piece, actually?"

"Nope, I'm afraid not."

"Do *not* say 'nope' to me. Do you know what 'nope' says to me? Do you know what it says? *'Fuck you'!*"

You could see regret and fear taking hold of Mr. Adams like a quick-moving set of clouds blowing in. He hung his head (he was, like many teachers, deeply theatrical), and when he raised it he said, "Sweet Cheeks. Thomas. Folks. You want a lesson in losing your cool, in why it's important to think before you speak?" He pointed at himself, at his own face. "I lost it. Shouldn't have said it. I'm owning up to it. My bad. Now, everybody ready to play? Let's pick up on . . . third line, right after the rests." Out of sympathy, or maybe just embarrassment at realizing that, for the moment, we had power over Mr. Adams, we lifted our instruments and played whatever piece it was with the kind of stiff attention we could usually only manage when the principal was in the room.

But Thomas was unshameable. He sat there now with his trumpet in his lap, not even pretending to play. Most of us (I, definitely) would have been trembling, and then would have gone home and practiced until our lips ached. But Thomas had actual confidence, actual contempt. What could Mr. Adams possibly do to him now? Thomas would never have to worry about being yelled at again.

The minutes after the bell, which we all spent disassembling our instruments and chatting and loudly closing and latching our cases, were always chaotic, but now they had an extra edge, because we were all hoping for some sort of final confrontation. Either Mr. Adams would apologize again, or Thomas would tell him that he was going right up to the principal's office. Mr. Adams, shuffling sheet music on the piano top, had the look of someone waiting for bad news.

But Thomas, with all our eyes on him, just clicked his case shut, stood up, and, for reasons I've never understood, turned to me. "Well," he said, "that could have worked out a lot worse, huh?" And he walked out into the hall.

That was, I think, the moment when he became interesting to me. I hadn't known there was any lightness in him, hadn't known that, along with his brain, he was set apart from the rest of us by a sense that what happened in school wasn't nearly so serious as we thought. I also hadn't known that there could be forms of rebellion subtler than setting your farts on fire or drawing boobs on the back of your hand. I put my drumsticks away and walked out of the room next to Thomas. I had an inkling (which I would give a considerable amount to go back and tell myself not to heed) that I may have had him entirely wrong.

The thing I wanted most, during my months of suffering over Claire (the thing other than Claire herself), was to be distracted, and for some reason the person who was best at distracting me was an eight-year-old tutee named Nicholas.

He lived on one of those absurdly beautiful cobblestone blocks in Georgetown, in a row house with a heavy front door that made it impossible to know whether your doorbell ring had sounded. My tutoring boss, an overcaffeinated woman named Barbara, had warned me that he'd scared off a couple of tutors before me, but by then I was accepting just about every assignment she offered, since it meant being out of the apartment.

A housekeeper, Maria, answered the door that first time, smiling to apologize for her English, and led me up the stairs. The house inside felt like a daguerreotype. There was a parlor with a pair of dark green couches and a giant chipping mirror over the mantel; all the windows ran on rusty chains; the floorboards had nails that kept snagging my socks. I thought that Nicholas's problem might be a kind of *Secret Garden* feebleness—withered legs, Victorian snottiness.

My first sight of him was as a snub-nosed face barely poking past the edge of a stars-and-comets blanket. "*Dios mío,*" Maria said, pulling the door closed behind her. When I said hi he growled, "*I hate tutors. Go away. Now,*" and turned to face the wall.

I sighed and sat down on his low red desk chair (for some reason I always overacted *Mr. Rogers*–ishly around kids that young), and said that I was sorry he was upset and that I'd be right here when he felt like doing some work.

"*I don't care.*"

"That's fine."

"*So go away!*"

After half an hour Maria came back in, folding a bath towel, and said, "Sorry, he no working today. You come Thursday, OK? I tell *papi.*"

Thursday was the same as Tuesday, and so was the Tuesday after that, so for three afternoons I sat at his miniature desk watching it get dark outside, drawing interlocking cubes on scratch paper. Boulder-like patience/indifference was one of the few benefits of my misery that fall. Sometimes Nicholas's little brother, Teddy, appeared in the doorway holding a half-built Lego airplane or a PSP, wanting to know if Nicholas would answer *one* tiny question. Sometimes Maria brought in the portable phone and it would be one of his parents, use-lessly insisting that he get up right this instant or else.

At some point on the fourth afternoon like this, he broke. A couple of times per session I'd been saying things like, "It's just too bad, because I was hoping someone could remind me who that *Star Wars* guy was with the red face and the little horns . . ." (his bed frame was covered in *Star Wars* stickers). Now, on a wet Thursday afternoon at the end of November, he finally said, in a voice that made clear that he was only calling a time-out from sulking, "Darth Maul."

"Hmm?"

"Darth Maul. The red guy's name is Darth Maul. And he's a Sith lord."

By the end of that afternoon he was sitting up, throwing

back his covers, asking if I'd hand him his binder of cards. He didn't hate tutors half as much as he hated the idea of someone going through life not knowing about the entire episodes of *Star Wars* that existed only as comic books.

By December he was pushing in front of Maria to meet me at the door, tugging my hand to get me up the stairs. He had blond-brown hair that went halfway down his neck and he wore long-sleeved T-shirts, little boy jeans, sneakers with lights in the soles; by high school he'd probably be an athlete. His problems turned out to be ADD, hyperactivity, ordinary private school stuff. We spent most of our time in his bedroom. Barbara didn't like her tutors working in bedrooms ("Even though I know, of course, that absolutely none of my tutors would *ever* . . ."), but with Nicholas I had no choice, because the downstairs was so dark and because his bedroom was where he kept his backpack and his supplies. So we worked side by side on our stomachs across his bed, chatting between problems like kids at a sleepover. He asked me if I'd ever killed anything and told me how, at his grandmother's in Florida, he'd once dropped a slug off a fifth-floor balcony. He asked me whether plants were immortal (meaning, he said, if there's ivy on the side of a building, is it the same ivy that was there a hundred years ago?). He told me how he was pretty sure that if people ever moved to space, he'd want to live on either Neptune or Pluto, since he hated hot weather. "Do you think we're kind of like best friends?" he said once. "I think the good thing about us is that we're cool but we're also smart."

There seemed to be no limit to the number of hours his parents, or at least his mother, were willing to hire me. I had my own key to their house by December, and they bought food I liked—Orange Milanos, Fruit Leathers—for the nights I babysat (even though babysitting was another thing that Barbara forbade her tutors to do, and even though I hadn't felt truly hungry since breaking up with Claire).

Nicholas and Teddy didn't notice or didn't care that I was

suffering, which may have been part of what made me suffer so much less around them. I would sit next to the two of them at the piano in their giant dark living room while they played "Heart and Soul," and though I couldn't quite bring myself to join them in stomping their feet, at some point I would think: *Hey, I haven't felt bad in minutes.* (Teddy, who was seven, had the personality of an aging Las Vegas diva. He'd come into the room wearing his mom's sunglasses and scarf and say, "Hello, sexies!" and then giggle and run down the hall while Nicholas chased him with a ruler.) For dinner we ate microwave pizza, which Nicholas and I would watch spin and bubble behind the dotted yellow window. We'd play Spy, sneaking around corners and pretending to shoot blowgun darts at each other. I felt like a father in a movie who has a terminal disease and doesn't tell his kids, so they can all just enjoy a few final weeks of happiness.

On one of these nights—the three of us were sitting cross-legged in a circle, playing Crazy Eights (this was the winter of card games)—Nicholas said, "I think my dad has a girlfriend now."

He said it in the clear, not-particularly-urgent way that someone who's just woken up from a nap on the beach might say, "We should go in or we're going to get burned."

"Really?" I said. "Why do you think that?"

"I don't know, he just talks about her a lot. And my mom says he does."

After that I started noticing that Anna was calling him "the boys' father" instead of Peter, and that more and more when she called me to babysit it was because she was going out for a girls' night. On her bedside table (I could see their room as I passed on the way up the stairs) there was a book called *Making the Transition: How to Survive (and Thrive) After a Separation.*

Peter had always looked to me like the kind of guy who, under his expensive watch and camel-hair trench coat, would be capable of real nastiness, maybe even violence. He made me think of a hyena. He'd hand me checks without looking at me, he'd drop the boys off without getting out of the car.

Anna was tall and pale with long dark hair that looked like it had never been cut, and apparently she worked for a nonprofit that had something to do with transportation alternatives. It was harder to imagine her in an office than in a club somewhere playing folk guitar—she was pretty, especially for someone close to forty, but it was the kind of prettiness that sometimes comes with a hint of BO or a streak of craziness (crystals, horses). She said to me, after one of those girls' nights when we were standing in the front hall, "You've lost someone, haven't you?"

"Hmm?"

"Did you lose someone? You've had that kind of . . . smashed look. How about a cup of tea?"

This was in January, a day or two after one of the blizzards we had that winter. I was happy to put off the half-block expedition to my car.

I couldn't tell if she was slightly drunk or just unguarded in the way that people sometimes get late at night; for some reason she made me think of an exhausted little girl playing house. We sat across from each other at the wooden table in their kitchen, waiting for the kettle to boil. Outside, the wind on the snow sounded like something trying to take off.

"How were they tonight? Were they OK?"

"They were good. Teddy didn't want to take a bath, but they were good."

"I'm sorry the house is like this. Half our stuff is still at Peter's mother's place." She rolled her eyes as if I'd know what she was talking about.

"I'm sorry if I freaked you out," she said, when she stood up to turn off the stove. "Asking you about losing someone?"

"You didn't freak me out. It's just girlfriend stuff. Or non-girlfriend stuff, I guess."

"That's kind of what I figured. It totally sucks, doesn't it? I feel like no one ever tells you. Or maybe you just can't believe it until it's you. My friends used to talk about getting separated and I'd be like, *Oh, OK, sorry*. But now just—*boom*. Like having some disease. Do you want milk?"

We both held our mugs with two hands and I kept looking down into the steam so I wouldn't have to meet her eyes. She asked me how long I'd been dating Claire, whether we'd been living together. She told me that she couldn't look at Nicholas sometimes now; he reminded her so much of Peter, just his face when he laughed, the way he held his chin when he read.

"Thanks so much for the tea," I kept saying, when I finally left, as if she'd brewed it from gold flakes.

She stood in the front doorway watching me make my way down the stairs (the snow on the ground had turned into what felt like hardened brown sugar), and I almost wanted to turn around and offer to spend the night: the thought of her alone with Nicholas and Teddy in that enormous dark house was too much. (Why was the thought of me alone in my crypt of a bedroom not too much? I don't know. For those few minutes, under the influence of the conversation or the snow or the ice pick–sharp stars, I felt like I didn't need anyone's pity.)

At home I stayed up in our apartment's only comfortable chair reading Chekhov's "The Black Monk" (having time to read was another of the benefits of my unhappiness), but before I'd gotten more than a couple of pages in, before I'd even met the black monk, I was falling asleep. I woke up, with the lamp blazing in my face, from a sex dream about Anna in which she was hovering over me and telling me, in a voice that somehow felt like clean sheets, to calm down, stop worrying, that she knew me, she knew everything about me, and all of it, believe her, was OK.

Thomas and I took the bus to his house that first afternoon, which already put me off balance. I'd ridden on city buses only a couple of times (in fact I'd gone around D.C. without an adult only a couple of times), so I felt, as I spilled what seemed to me like every coin in my backpack into the bus driver's silver trough, that I was doing something obviously wrong.

"Do you ride this every day?"

"More or less."

"Is it always this crowded?"

"Usually it is."

I felt, irritatingly, a desire to impress him, and on his terms. I wished I'd prepared by reading a book about World War II, or by coming up with some intriguing questions about my stepdad's new computer.

His house turned out to be on one of the steep streets in Cleveland Park near the zoo. The sidewalks were broken up by huge gray roots and instead of lawns these houses had ivy and terraces. These were the kinds of neighborhoods, I learned later, in which adults were always bragging about running into old secretaries of defense and directors of the OMB at the hardware store or the Chinese place.

Thomas let us in (using a key that hung on a nail under the porch, which seemed to me another adult touch) and I was struck almost at once by a feeling I hadn't had in years. There are certain places, certain objects, that seem in some hard-to-explain way alive, and that give a weird charmed quality to everything you do in them or with them. When I was little I seemed to get this feeling more regularly; it would come over me when I was holding a glass, or wearing a particular sweater, or sitting in the unpainted corner of the kitchen in one of the first apartments I remember. Warmth? Happiness? Home? What comes to mind is the way wood sometimes looks in sunlight; there's a Vermeer-ish quality to what I'm talking about. Anyway, the Pells' house had it.

Aside from this feeling, and a general attic kind of smell, the sound of his house's floors is what struck me most vividly. They creaked with every step anyone took, this deep, almost cartoonish sound. And the walls of the living room were covered, absolutely covered, with books: the seven-volume complete works of Freud, the notebooks of Tolstoy, the letters of Virginia Woolf, on and on and on (none of these names meant anything to me, but I was very impressed with the sight of a real library; this, I figured, was what he did with himself while I was watching back-to-back episodes of *The Fresh Prince*).

And underneath all this was the fact that his parents weren't home, that no adult was. I knew enough not to mention it, but it was as impressive and unusual as if we'd come in and there had been a pet tiger roaming around (in fact there was a pet cat, Vladimir, who wove around my legs as if he were trying to tie my shoelaces together). I was used to people's houses in the afternoons: being drearily hovered over by mothers who wanted to relieve the loneliness of their days by making us grilled-cheese sandwiches, or by housekeepers who couldn't pretend not to mind seeing footprints and backpacks on their just-cleaned floors. To get away you'd have to close yourself in a bedroom, where you'd look at someone's Magic 8 Ball and wait for the sound of footsteps in the hall.

But Thomas was an adult in the way only children some-times become adults. As soon as we walked in he went to the kitchen and made us a chicken breast in a pan with tomato sauce poured on top; we sat side by side at the high coun-ter eating, while he sorted through a stack of mail as if there might be a bill or a magazine for him.

"Do you want to . . . see the backyard?" he said afterward. This led to a few minutes of wandering through the bamboo, peering through the fence at a neighbor's dog licking himself. "Should we go up to my room?" In his room we sat on his bed and he showed me a book of old *New Yorker* cartoons, some of which were racy in a way I could hardly understand; I half smiled in case he wanted me to laugh. A truth was slowly making its way through me, like heat through a cold house: Thomas had no idea how to have someone over. The worry was not all mine. He must have figured that something would just happen if you put two people together in playdate conditions, but here it was, not happening.

"I hope you don't think it's weird," he finally said, "that I invited you over." By then we were downstairs in front of the TV (Thomas scanned through the channels with the arrows rather than the numbers, giving himself away as an amateur).

"No. Why would it be weird?"

"I don't really have people over. I always think they wouldn't have any fun." He paused for long enough that I thought he might have been waiting for me to say that *of course* people would have fun. But he said, "If I ask you some-thing, do you promise you won't tell anyone at school?"

"OK."

"I feel like I should ask you to swear to God. Do you believe in God?"

"No, not really."

"Me neither. Well, I'll just trust you then."

Like everyone who insists on how trustworthy they are, or maybe just like everyone, I broke promises constantly, but I was determined to know Thomas's secret. Maybe he wanted me to join him in committing the perfect murder, maybe he was actually forty-five years old.

No: he wanted to know if I thought there was any way Michelle Koller liked him.

I was lucky to have the TV to look at while I considered this. It wasn't the thought of Michelle liking him that was absurd (although it was), but the thought of him, reader of *Hamlet,* expert on the Treaty of Versailles, liking Michelle; so this was what was going on all day inside that famous head.

"You went to her party a few weeks ago, didn't you?" he said, talking faster now. "Did you see her room? What are her parents like?" A few minutes later: "I wanted to ask Rebecca about her, but I couldn't get her alone."

Michelle was the leader of a group of girls—a group that included my girlfriend, Rebecca—who were collectively known for their hotness. They were a kind of chorus, with a girl at every pitch (Alice, tall and muscular, was the baritone; Rebecca, tiny and dainty, was the soprano). And Michelle was like the note you get when you rub a wet fingertip on crystal: she floated above varieties and was just sort of the thing itself.

"Has Rebecca ever said anything about me liking Michelle? I'm worried she knows."

"No," I said honestly. Rebecca had hardly ever said anything at all.

Anyway, the caste system is strict in middle school—I was just at the edge of what my status allowed with Rebecca—and Thomas had no more chance of dating Michelle Koller than he did Michelle Pfeiffer. Still, I did my best to look serious as he showed me a Valentine's Day card he'd made and then not given to her, and the couple of pages of surprisingly good sketches he'd made of her sitting at her desk, her hair behind her ears.

I gave him advice, like a stock picker with a dupe for a client. It turned out not to matter after all that I couldn't remember which side Russia had been on in World War II. Tell her you like her sweater, I said. Ask her if she needs help with her homework. Leave mix tapes on her desk. Try to be the last person to say good-bye to her at the end of each day.

And each of these little dramas, although they of course weren't going to lead anywhere, gave us something to talk over afterward at his house. I liked being the kid who'd cracked Thomas Pell; it was like having learned to communicate with an owl. First I'd go over once a week, maybe twice. By May we didn't even have to ask what the other was doing—we'd walk out of school together and head straight for the bus stop. I'd come to like him more than I liked the people who used to laugh at my impressions of him. Soon we were having sleepovers in his bedroom with its bookshelves and slanted ceilings; we were making up names for people at school and making up words for things we didn't want to be overheard talking about; I was eating dinner at his house so often that his mom would set a place for me without asking.

But throughout all this, he remained gloomily obsessed with Michelle. I hadn't read *The Great Gatsby* yet, but this was pure Gatsby and Daisy: tragic longing, obsessive planning.

At the end of that first May of our friendship there was a grade-wide field trip to the aquarium in Baltimore. This meant signing permission slips, getting to school at seven thirty in the morning, climbing onto an old-apple-juice-smelling bus. Thomas and I had come up with a plan that Thomas was going to sidle up to Michelle at some point in the afternoon, probably in a dark exhibit, and try putting his arm around her. I knew this was hopelessly, ridiculously creepy, but Thomas and I had spent a couple of afternoons at his house, standing at his bedroom window and pretending it was an aquarium tank, practicing how he'd ease his arm up her back and around her shoulders.

We were in the Amazon River Basin Gallery when he told me that it wasn't working. "I tried to get near her and she used Alice to scrape me off. I think she might be upset with me. Or just in a bad mood."

"No, try in the next exhibit. See? In one of the little dark hallways."

He closed his eyes and nodded, and I watched as he spent the next five minutes slowly following her around between the jellyfish tanks, edging his way close to her, looking like someone trying to pick her pocket.

He came back over to me and said, "Well, that was an Arc de Triomphe," which was what we said when something had gone wrong. On the bus ride home we sat next to each other not talking, and it occurred to me, watching miles of those beige sound-blocking walls, that he might finally have realized how hopeless he was, and that now might be the time to admit that he was right. "Beetlejuice, Beetlejuice, Beetlejuice" was all I could think to say, which was another of our words for failure (our language, it's occurring to me now, was especially rich on this subject).

Once it started to get dark outside, and once the teachers and chaperones had all begun either falling asleep or sinking into a post-field-trip state of not giving a shit, a game of Truth or Dare developed. Paul Wolham rubbed his penis against the window and pretended he'd had an orgasm. Lauren Langer had to say whether she'd ever had a sex dream. John Swider had to go to the front of the bus and ask the driver if there was anywhere on board to poop.

I could see where this was going. Being friends with Thomas was like being friends with an alcoholic; chances to creep out Michelle were his liquor stores, his bars. He and I went back to join the game just after Michelle and Rebecca did. By then Rebecca and I may have been breaking up; anyway we didn't acknowledge each other.

It was Alex Rozmarin, this spastic red-haired kid, who finally dared Michelle to kiss Thomas. There are no secret crushes in middle school; Thomas's hopelessness was becoming as public a fact as his intelligence.

It wasn't a fact for him, though. He turned toward her and

raised his eyebrows in a way that said, *Well? Here I am, and I guess we're going to have to do this, aren't we?*

She didn't move and she wasn't (it was as clear as if she'd said it) even thinking about it. "Truth," she said. "I choose truth."

"You said dare!" Alex shrieked. "You can't go back! You have to kiss Thomas!"

But he was overruled. Thomas stayed standing but now he'd turned his face away from Michelle, down toward the floor, and he seemed to be shrinking inward, like a burning leaf. In the look that had come over her at the thought of having to kiss him, he'd finally seen the truth. If the bus's back door had been open I think he would have flung himself out.

Instead (and this was, I think, when I first noticed his inclination toward emotional seppuku) he looked up, as if he'd heard a whistle in the distance. In his clearest, most measured voice, he said, "Michelle, I've made you uncomfortable, and I apologize. I shouldn't have come back here. I should have accepted what was obvious a long time ago. You won't need to worry about avoiding me anymore. I'll never bother you again."

On a Saturday a week or so after the tea with Anna, I took Nicholas and Teddy ice-skating in the Sculpture Garden at the National Gallery. This was a dripping, dishrag-gray day, and I was feeling mildly poisoned not only because of the weather but because I thought I'd seen Claire in the crowd that afternoon at Metro Center. The changing room smelled like wet socks and dirty rubber. As I kneeled in front of a bench, tying Nicholas's skates, he said, "You're kind of like our dad now, huh?"

For some reason this added to my gloom, and without looking up I said, "No, your dad's your dad. I'm just your friend. Now give me your other foot."

Teddy, standing balanced with one hand on my head, asked if he could go get a soft pretzel (he was always in a panic about when he was going to eat next), and I knocked his arm away, stood up, told them to quit being so slow or else I was going to take them home. I spent the hour on the ice dropping their hands, telling them they needed to learn to stay up on their own, doing everything I could not to look like their father. Beatles songs played on a loop out of faraway-sounding speakers and backward-skating show-offs zoomed around and between us.

"Can we stop for bagels on the way home?" Teddy asked, while we were hobbling back into the locker room.

"No."

"Are you mad at us?"

"No. Not if you take your skates off and go get your shoes."

I must have already known that I was going to start sleeping with their mother. When I try now to pinpoint the first moment when I realized this might actually happen, it keeps getting pushed earlier. Yes, the night of the tea, the dream, but hadn't there been weird looks, little pauses, before then? Joel used to call her my middle-aged mistress, when I'd stand talking to her on the phone at night—he'd once dated an older woman, and he talked about it like an exotic dish he'd once eaten on vacation, something everyone should try before they die.

Anyway, a few days after the skating Anna left me a message (she always left me a couple of messages a week, asking if I could babysit an extra night or stay after to tutor Teddy), saying that she wondered if we could grab coffee sometime to talk about Nicholas. He'd gotten in a fight at school, apparently, and this wasn't new, but this latest one was especially bad. There were a couple of kids in his class who called him "the Dick," poured Pixy Stix in his hair, and he was incapable of backing down or shutting up—he was the kind of kid who'd keep shouting even as the teacher dragged him away with a bloody nose (he was also the kind of kid whose nose bled if you tapped it). She worried, she said, that with everything going on with his dad he'd keep acting out more and more and she was just about out of ideas. She wasn't working Wednesday afternoon, if there was any way she could steal me for an hour.

We met at a coffee shop on Wisconsin just after four, when it was already almost dark. It had been raining so long that the sun seemed possibly to have gone out altogether. I'd spent the day researching law schools, which had meant mostly writing emails and watching old episodes of *Family Ties* on YouTube. There were only a few other people with us in the café, which had kids' crayon drawings all over the walls and butcher-paper tablecloths. A classical radio station that sounded like falling asleep was playing, and in the corner a woman was breast-feeding with a kind of amazing lack of self-consciousness. The one waiter drifted around grumpily, forgetting to bring sugar, checking his phone. We didn't talk about Nicholas at first—instead we talked about a friend of hers at work who'd started beekeeping, a new Spanish restaurant in Friendship Heights. We both had big ceramic mugs of weak coffee and we made a show, to the waiter's indifference, of deciding whether we wanted something sweet. Finally we settled on sharing a slice of German chocolate cake, which I ended up eating most of and she ended up pretending to have eaten most of.

"It's so nice talking to someone who actually *knows* the boys. I get almost greedy about it. Would you tell me if I was too much?"

"You're not too much."

"Well, you're sweet. How have you been?"

Something about Anna made me able to talk about Claire without sounding, I think, like someone who lies in bed at night with his heart pounding, wondering what went wrong—instead I could say things like, "Well, I think I'm about done licking my wounds," as if I were describing the aftermath of a tough game of cricket.

"Whoever does end up with you is going to be seriously lucky," she said.

"Oh, I don't know about that."

"I'm serious! You're a total catch."

Too-frank compliments can have an effect on a conversation like too-frank insults. We hadn't said much for a minute when the waiter brought the check, and when we finally started to stand up she said, "I love these afternoons when they both have lessons," and that, if I had to pick a moment, was when it was decided. In the corner the woman was still breast-feeding, this white veiny watermelon hanging out, and that may have had something to do with the mood too. I pretended I was walking up the block with her because I felt like getting some fresh air (the rain had picked up again); she pretended this sounded reasonable. Within fifteen minutes we were together on her large white bed, my jeans were around my ankles before my shoes were off, my coat was on the floor in the corner of the room, the lights were on, we were making the noises that people make, she was whispering the things that people whisper. I was distracting myself by trying to make words out of the letters in *middle-aged mistress.*

This, I thought, tugging a bra strap here, feeling myself yanked and squeezed there, *is actually what's happening! The person who this morning couldn't stop thinking about Claire is right now scrambling around on his knees, reaching across to . . .*

Afterward I settled down with my head on her chest. We'd known what we were doing, apparently.

"See?" she said. "I told you people would want you."

She petted my head and I looked around the room, thinking of Nicholas running out of that bathroom in his Cars pajamas with his hair still wet. The radiator pipes knocked and knocked. Anna smelled not at all bad but very noticeably like skin and sweat and person. I looked into the dark window next to the bed and thought, *Cold* (in fact there were now goose bumps all along my arms and legs) *but not alone.* My heart seemed to have become slow and loud and enormous, as if I'd just come out of a long bath.

I told her I needed to get home to get ready for another appointment, which wasn't true, but I did suddenly feel that I had to get away before what we'd done could catch up with us. Dressing in front of her somehow seemed much more intimate and embarrassing than having sex with her. "Do you want to borrow an umbrella?" she said. She watched me sleepily from the bed and beckoned me over (making me think, very much against my will, of an old lady calling to her children from her deathbed). "Don't drive yourself crazy," she said. "We're adults." She kissed me on the forehead.

Driving home I didn't feel crazy, exactly; I felt the way I'd felt after losing my virginity in high school, this strobe light flashing between pride and disbelief. And I thought, like a mantra, *Keep moving, keep moving, keep moving.* A woman came out of her house with her two fat huskies. A boy in a Curious George poncho ran ahead of a mom who was carrying a yoga mat and groceries. Was it really, for the rest of the world, just a regular Wednesday afternoon? Didn't anyone know or care what I'd been doing? A police car stopped behind me at a red light and I thought for a half heartbeat they might be pulling me over.

By the time I went to bed that night (having gone into the bathroom a few times to check for evidence, having not thought about Claire for whole half hours at a time), I'd decided, first, that I would never tell anyone, including Joel, and second, that this would only happen once, and that if Anna tried to arrange something again I would tell her that she was beautiful and wonderful but that it was just too weird and sorry.

No and no and no. It didn't work like that at all.

———————

As I'm remembering my friendship with Thomas, it's hard not to stop here, to plant a flag on the spot in my life when problems meant embarrassments and when I couldn't imagine someone not being able to sleep through the night. But memory's like a six-year-old: And then? And then? And then?

By that summer Thomas and I were best friends in the society-of-two, not-necessarily-cheerful way that sometimes happens with kids that age. We had sleepovers every weekend, we spent afternoons walking the bike trail behind his house. My mom sometimes asked me, not quite suppressing her worry, what it was we did in all that time we spent together. At first she'd been thrilled that I'd found a best friend—she'd been in a more or less perpetual state of nervous guilt about having made me leave my school in Baltimore—but maybe she'd seen a *Dateline* special on troublesome teens, or maybe my stepdad, Frank, had muttered something to her; she may even have worried that we were gay. We weren't, of course—our desire to find girlfriends was one of the foundations of our friendship—but even if I'd wanted to explain to her why we spent so much time together, I couldn't really have done it in any way that would have made sense to her. Adult friendship is all talking and laughing and bickering and planning; teenage friendship can be more of a joined solitude, like oxen yoked together. The not-having-to-do-anything can be the whole point.

"You're going to be happier than I am in high school," Thomas said to me one day. "I don't seem to have the courage to disappoint my parents, which seems like a crucial ingredient."

By then he knew everything about my family: about my parents having gotten divorced when I was one; about my mom's years of dating (which I remembered mostly as her frizz of red-dyed hair and a parade of nervous men handing me toy trucks or Nerf footballs, as if I were a baby chimp). He knew about the awkwardness of my stepdad, who I often thought I could stump by asking him my middle name, and about Frank's son, Ian, who I knew only from a handful of trips home from Wash U, during which he drank weight-gainer shakes and showed me naked pictures of his girlfriend. I knew, of course, that when I told Thomas all this I was selling out my family, but I didn't care. My family was like the cardboard *Apollo* astronauts outside Blockbuster—you could sweep them aside, fold them into the Dumpster, without thinking about it.

Halfway along the bike trail there was a homeless encampment—clotheslines and a fire pit and a few half-empty water jugs—that we liked to poke around in, imagining that we heard people coming. For some reason this was where we always had our best and frankest talks—about whether happiness was more valuable than intelligence; about whether women really cared about penis size; about the neighbor of mine with OCD who'd swum laps until the lifeguards had dragged him out of the pool. We called these talks *symposiums,* which was a word I'd learned from Thomas. We really thought that we might, sitting there past sunset, picking up used condoms with sticks (these were the first condoms I'd ever seen, and at first I took them for some kind of food wrapper), solve the problems that had been troubling humans since the beginning of time.

Symposiums were also often when Thomas's version of a wild side came out—not the kind of wildness the bad kids at school had, breaking things and pulling down their pants, but the kind of wildness woods had: he turned strange, indifferent, a little dark. "I'm not sure I feel a lot of the things that you're supposed to," he said once. "Except for you and my parents, I'm not sure whose death I'd actually care much about."

(My biological dad, who lived in Tucson and who I'd seen only a handful of times in the past decade, happened to die that summer. He had a heart attack while he was playing tennis with his girlfriend. My mom woke me up buzzing with the news, as if she'd been plugged into some sort of charge; she seemed to expect me to act upset, so I did. I only felt capable of figuring out how I actually felt about it—mostly annoyed that everyone thought I must be devastated—once I could talk to Thomas.)

At the homeless encampment, Thomas liked to pile leaves and garbage into the fire pit, which was just a ring of stones, and then light them with matches that he'd taken from one of the restaurants near where the bus let out on Connecticut. The fires burned blue, orange, white, gave off stinking curls of oily smoke; he'd watch and take a couple of seconds to respond to whatever I said to him. "I think I'd like to be cremated," he said. "Fire seems like the best state that matter can aspire to."

One afternoon a park worker (we called him a police officer when we told the story to each other afterward) stepped through the trees just as one of these fires was as its peak, and once I'd started to run, my body clanging with disaster, I looked back and saw that Thomas hadn't followed me—he was walking calmly in the other direction. I hid behind a tree, too far to hear what Thomas and the officer were saying to each other, but I imagined that Thomas had had an inner collapse and that he was turning himself in. I'd make my way home alone.

But he came strolling over, not with the officer, and as we walked back to his house he told me, sounding almost bored with the need to explain, what he'd said. "My friend and I were out walking along the path and we thought we saw a fire burning, so we ran over to put it out but we couldn't find any water."

And like that: resolved. I was slightly, silently mad at him for the rest of the afternoon for being so much better than me at coping in an emergency. The practical world was supposed to be my realm.

When we weren't in the woods, we spent most of our time at the Pells' house, despite my mom's pleading. I knew she'd embarrass me in front of Thomas; I knew Frank would want to take us to the country club, where he'd turn red in the sauna and fart like a silverback gorilla. The few sleepovers we had at my house felt like exhibition games; whatever fun we managed was halfhearted and conditional.

And as I got to know his parents, I began to feel that way about my house even when I wasn't with Thomas. When my mom and I had first moved into Frank's, just before seventh grade, I'd felt like the kid on *Silver Spoons*—my new bedroom was the size of our old living room; the kitchen had two dishwashers and two sinks; in the backyard there was a little heated pool hidden by a hedge where Frank liked to float on Saturday afternoons. But now that I knew the Pells, now that I'd seen the look on Thomas's face as Frank showed us how to turn on the jets, it all seemed pathetic, like a *SkyMall* catalog you could live inside. Could the Pells' dim, golden dining room really exist just a few miles from this one with its fake fruit and stacks of *Time* magazine? My mom and Frank, the house, their whole lives, seemed now like a microwavable meal, plastic wrapped and artificially colored.

Thomas's mom, Sally, sometimes asked polite questions about what it was like having a mom who was a pharmacist ("She must be just wonderful when you have the flu"), but I knew that they could never be friends, that they could never even really have a conversation, and I knew that Sally knew it too. She practiced some sort of law that was the opposite of my stepdad's; she was always talking about fraud and city agencies and the lobbyists who actually wrote our legislation. She carried binders and tote bags. She might have been the only mom I knew with undyed gray hair. She'd taken to calling out both Thomas's and my names as soon as she walked in the door. "Well, don't you two look comfortable!" Her accent (she was from Georgia) made everything she said sound as if she were curtsying. "I was thinking about steak tonight—sound all right by you two?"

"Mm-hmm."

"Adam, you check with your folks?"

"They don't mind!"

"Why not go ahead and give 'em a call, just to be sure."

"OK!"

I'd never been around an adult who seemed actually to like me; not to love me, in the smothering and depressing and animal way my mom did, and not to feign interest in me, in the professional, blank-eyed way my teachers did, but actually to want to sit down and hear what I had to say about something. Sally would pour herself a glass of white wine and, while Thomas sat at his computer in the other room, say to me, "So, did they let y'all out to watch the verdict? Everyone in my office was gathered around a portable TV like it was a campfire." Or she might ask me what I thought about the idea of seventy-minute periods, which the high school had just decided to try out. I had no practice in sitting at a table and coming up with opinions; it felt like learning to sing.

"Mom?" Thomas would call out without looking away from the computer. "What are you talking about?"

"Oh, we're just gossiping in here." And then sometimes she'd say (I loved to hear this the way a cat loves having its back stroked), "Adam, I just love to talk to you. If Thomas was in charge I think I'd just slide his meals under the door and come get him when Richard gets home."

A lot of Sally's liking me, I knew, had to do with my influence on Thomas; she was happier to see him finally with a best friend than he was. Even the parents of a boy like Thomas,

parents who are confident that their son will one day in the
not too distant future write books and invent cures and design
cathedrals, even they're secretly worried that he spends too
much time alone. And of course Thomas did, pre-me, spend
huge amounts of time alone. At his computer he'd stare into
games that seemed to consist of geometric figures shooting
each other, pyramids sliding toward rectangles, beeping. He
read for hours at a sitting. Never once do I remember him
putting music on just to have it on; it would have been as
weird as if he'd one day put on a Santa hat.

But I'm putting off describing Thomas's dad, Richard. I
have a sense, like someone trying to describe Michelangelo's
David, that I won't be able to get any of the important parts
of him onto the page. This would sound strange, maybe even
crazy, to someone who was just meeting him for the first time;
all you'd see would be a not particularly tall, ordinarily handsome, suburban D.C. dad in his forties, proud of his posture,
serious about his handshake. But he had, if you stood close to
him, a shimmer that certain people have, a kind of celebrity
extra-reality, as if he existed both where you were with him
and in movies or on newsclips. When I read *The Odyssey,* that
first year of high school, it was Richard I always imagined as
Odysseus—and I wasn't the least bit surprised when Thomas
told me that he was doing the same thing.

Richard wore jeans, T-shirts, sweaters, plaid shirts with
the sleeves rolled up. Later, when I was in my early twenties, I
realized that the style I was going for, the look I had whenever
I most approved of what I saw in the mirror, was Richard's.
He had a pink bald head and close-set, Doberman-ish eyes.
He was as thin as Thomas, but he was athletic—he was the
only dad I knew who worked out, though his working out
actually wasn't anything like what we (or people slightly older
than us) did. He ran; every morning you could find him out
before sunrise, floating along the edge of Connecticut, wearing
weightless clothes and white Reeboks battered brown. He also
rowed, alone, out on the Potomac. Until seeing him I hadn't

known that this was a sport, but there he was on this boat that looked, with his oars going and himself sliding up and down, up and down, like some sort of floating insect. Racing into a V of ripples, disappearing under bridges, while Thomas and I walked alongside onshore. At home he did chin-ups on the bar between the kitchen and the front hall, what seemed to me countless at the time but really couldn't have been any more than, what, twenty? I imagined that he would have been capable of tearing up railroad ties or punching through doors. In one of my most vivid memories of him, Thomas is hanging from his legs and Richard isn't slowed down in the least; you'd only know he was having to do any extra work at all by the slight smile that joined his usual workout expression.

Even at twelve, thirteen years old I understood: I wanted him to be my father. And he was, to an extent that couldn't possibly have delighted me more, up for the job. He was a teacher. Not just literally (he taught about the Civil War at Georgetown) but in terms of temperament, inclinations. He knew things. He attracted disciples. I couldn't talk to him for five minutes without learning some astonishing thing, some way of thinking, that I wouldn't be able to wait to misquote as my own.

For instance:

"The early Christians, the people who were coming up with this stuff, they weren't going to movies, they weren't living in cities. They were farmers. Farmers of what in particular? Grapes. And you've probably never seen grapes grow, but the plant is this hideous, gnarly thing, like a hand with arthritis. And the grapes come up, and then they vanish. Just leaving the hand again. And then back they come the next season. And so what did these people, watching the holy life—because a crop to a farmer is holy—birth and death, birth and death, come up with? Resurrection. Reembodiment. Lazarus. Christ was a crop. He has risen."

Or:

"So there's impression, the buzz of sensory data, and the

mind says, *Sir, yes, sir,* and constructs a world, a story, fits it all together, hides the circuitry. Which people think ends as a dorm room chew toy: is my green your green, OK, boring, got it. But now neuroscience is saying, What if the you who thinks he gets it is a story too? What if 'you' are just the face your mind makes out of the disconnected dots? Have you ever seen a Chuck Close?"

After dinner, once Sally had gone back into the living room, I would sit at the table with Thomas and Richard, silently sucking on what I had to say, what I'd been planning to say for the past ten minutes, wondering whether it would, in some way I couldn't forecast, reveal me as not having understood what they were talking about.

But when I'd finally hold my breath and come out with it—my question about why, if Catholics believed so much in the life of the fetus, they didn't hold funerals for miscarriages, or my idea about how the American colonists could have rationalized what they did to the Indians—Richard would, almost without fail, respond in such a way as to convince me, for as long as we were talking, that I was every bit as smart as Thomas, that my brain too was a rare burden. "'Ignorance is not an excuse.' That's very, very good. Wow. I may have to use that."

Sally sometimes sang in the other room, and Richard would stop talking to listen, and close his eyes, as if he were about to sneeze. One night, alarmingly, he said, "*Jesus,* I love that woman."

"I think my parents have a lot of sex," Thomas said once when we were walking along the bike path. "Like a *lot.*"

I didn't understand at the time that this was a kind of bragging, or if I did understand, it didn't bother me, because I felt that the glow of it included me. "Adam," Sally said one night, "pretty soon we're going to get so we're just going to fill out adoption papers for you. Your mom and I may just have a tug-of-war."

———

Anna and I met again that Friday afternoon, while Nicholas and Teddy were over at friends' houses (she answered the door in a blue silk kimono). On Sunday when they were with their father. The next Wednesday during music lessons. We were like teenagers.

We had sex against doors and on closet floors and in not-yet-entirely-warm baths. We were nearly caught by the UPS man. We took turns in the shower. She claimed to be dazzled by my young mannish stamina, which made me feel, for the first time in at least a year, as if I might actually still be young.

"What year were you born?" she said.

"Eighty-two."

"Wow. OK."

"You?"

"Sixty-nine. I know women are supposed to lie or something, but I don't really care. I'm kind of proud of it."

One afternoon she said, "You know, I think Peter was always jealous of you. I'm serious! I don't think he liked having a younger guy around."

She did turn out to have a streak of craziness (she flipped straight to the horoscopes, she didn't believe in flu shots) but she also had a streak of hardness, the kind of personality that settlers have, women who till fields with guns strapped to their backs.

She'd grown up in Vermont with just her mother, a school librarian, and three older brothers. She'd never had female friends, because they made her feel feral, with their creams and polishes. Instead she had boyfriends: she was the girl who'd let you practice taking off her bra, who'd explain how to know if a girl was faking. She'd gone to Johns Hopkins for college and then spent a couple of years trying to become a children's book illustrator (she showed me some of her old notebooks, and her drawings were better than I'd feared; cats somehow given personalities in three strokes, trees with old men's faces in their bark).

She'd met Peter through a friend at a fancy firm (he was an associate, five years older) and they'd only dated for nine months before he proposed; he seemed so serious and hopeful, she didn't want to hurt his feelings by saying no. She said that while she walked down the aisle, literally as she was holding her bouquet, trying not to stumble in her heels, she was thinking, *This is a mistake, this is a mistake.* She got pregnant with Nicholas just over a year later.

"This isn't the first one of these for you, is it?" I said.

She pursed her lips. "No. Is that a problem?"

"I don't think so."

"Tell me if you start thinking you might get hurt," she said. "I feel like I'm responsible for you. We're all happiness all the time, OK?"

I didn't think I'd get hurt (though I also couldn't really see how this would end well). Mostly I didn't think about it at all. Instead I kept tutoring Nicholas and Teddy—often on the same nights that I slept with their mother—and while I was with them Nicholas would say, "My mom said I can get an Xbox for my birthday," and the woman I thought of when he said this wouldn't be the same at all as the one who'd been clawing at my neck a few hours earlier.

Bit by bit I learned about the men before me, probably more than I should have. There was Andrew, the polite, nervous father of a boy in Teddy's class, who had eventually asked her to run away with him. And Max, the dumb, handsome guy who worked at the coffee shop in Tenleytown, who performed freestyle rap. Was there really this entire world of affairs bubbling away? Was that the great secret business of adulthood, the way alcohol and parties were the secret business of adolescence?

I kept my resolution about not telling anyone, almost. It was March before I told Joel (by then he'd seen a condom in my bag) and he said, "Are you serious? You're serious?! Holy shit. Ho-ly shit. Are her pubes gray? Wait, why are you wearing condoms?" That night at a bar he made a toast "to Anna, the cougar who brought my friend back to life," and the strangers next to us roared and clinked our glasses.

I did imagine, periodically, telling Claire about her, and a couple of times I even started typing an email (leaving the *"To:"* line blank, in case I sneezed or some craziness overtook me).

> You should know I'm thinking about you less than I have since we broke up, and feeling much better than I was. I've started sleeping with the mother of one of my tutees, which is not exactly the rebound I had in mind, but what I've come to think about happiness is . . .

I stopped myself and deleted it unsent, but I really was feeling better than I'd thought I would. Sleazy, yes, guilty and jumbled and occasionally in a kind of panic, but also awake; I had enough energy now to go for runs along K Street some mornings (there were still, somehow, patches of gray snow on most of the curbs), and my appetite was back, even if it pushed me mostly in the direction of eating chocolate chips and Saltines while standing at the kitchen counter in my gym shorts.

Not since first discovering masturbation had I overused myself quite like I did with Anna in those months. I felt like a wrung-out washcloth. It was as if we were conducting some sort of experiment, as if we'd been sent to keep each other from ever getting anything done. I hadn't thought about law school in I didn't know how long. I hadn't done laundry in so many weeks that I had to take socks and underwear from Joel's dresser. I would have said that I wasn't much of a tutor before, but now I'd go through whole appointments without opening my mouth to do more than yawn.

"How long do you think we can keep going like this?" Anna said once.

"I have no idea. We should be submitting records to Guinness."

"What do we do if we fall in love?"

"More or less what we're doing," I said, pushing her bedroom door shut.

I had rarely in my life been more certain that what I was doing was foolish, and I had never cared so little. At Nicholas's birthday party, during which a horde of boys raced around the house waving lightsabers, Anna pulled me into the guest bedroom and kissed me with lips that tasted like ice-cream cake. On a Sunday in April, when the weather was on its annual campaign to make D.C. seem not just habitable but glorious, we hid behind a tree off the Billy Goat Trail and, while I peeled off her shirt, I whispered that I loved her. Maybe I *did* love her, I thought. Maybe love didn't have to be so complicated and bloody; maybe "I love you" could be not much more than a sexual exclamation, a way of expressing happiness and disbelief.

But then the strangest thing happened, as suddenly as an attack of hay fever: I got jealous.

It started, I think, when I asked her one day (we were getting dressed in her bedroom, she was brushing her hair in front of the closet mirror) what was the longest that one of her affairs had ever lasted. She thought for a few more seconds than I would have liked and said, "I think with Max it was like five months."

I made a noise that apparently conveyed something pathetic, because she came over and cradled my head. "I never liked him half as much as I like you. He was full of himself."

That night when I was home, and for the next couple of days afterward, I found myself returning to the thought of Max like a loose tooth. He'd watched her clasp her bra, just the way I had. He'd felt the notches on her spine and the pale fuzz at the bottom of her back.

"What's wrong?" she said the next time we were together. "You're not kissing me normal."

And it was true: I wasn't doing anything normal. I had a miserable new pastime. On the afternoons I wasn't with her, when I usually went to the bookstore/coffee shop near my apartment to sit with my laptop, I found myself going to the one where Max worked in Tenleytown. She'd pointed him out to me once that March—she'd made us cross the street—and at the time he'd meant nothing to me, or if he had meant anything it was what a conquered people mean to their conqueror: *Look at him scuttling along!* But now that seemed impossible.

Now I watched him replacing the milk in the fridge, ringing people up, leaning on the counter reading *Black Book,* and I seethed with the private insanity of an assassin. I performed Google searches in the idiotic hope of learning his last name. I watched him get into his car (green Camry, COEXIST bumper sticker), and one afternoon, before shame or sanity stopped me, I even started to follow him.

A large part of the problem was that he was, in just about every measurable way, more attractive than me. I say this now as if it were a sad but simple fact, but at the time I felt as if my entire future depended on my finding an angle from which it wouldn't be true. He was definitely taller and stronger than me; that was a lost cause. But there had to be things I had over him, didn't there? Maybe something about my eyes? My stomach dropped the first time I heard that he had a slight southern accent (he was instructing a customer—wrongly!—on the fastest way to the Tidal Basin). He was Texan, I learned, after I'd overheard two women in the same day ask in just the same scarcely-controlling-themselves voices where he was from.

He was long without being quite lanky; his forearms were the forearms of someone with a gym membership. But there was a delicacy to him too, the little bit of stubble on his cheeks, the strands of black hair that hung over his eyebrows. He looked like someone who'd talk to you about the global food system, or how he was trying to phase plastic out of his life. Once in a while he wore a little flat-brimmed black canvas hat, which I wanted someone to join me in laughing at.

And he had tattoos. Tattoos! (Had Anna ever kissed them? Had he given her a tattoo-by-tattoo tour?) I was consumed for the better part of a morning in figuring out what the one on his left arm was—if it could only be something moronic, then I felt that I would finally be vindicated. A wheel? A ship's steering wheel? Was it a naval thing—maybe he was from a Texas military family? Or was it the kind of wheel where each spoke represents a different realm of reality, and at the center is your desire to demonstrate that you once spent three weeks in Tibet?

I'm not sure there's any emotion worse for you than jealousy. Anger, sadness, pity—even at their worst, they have a kind of purity to them: you're suffering but you're righteous, the world is failing to cooperate. But jealousy, oh, what a shameful and wincing performance. You're not just suffering; you're afraid of being exposed for your suffering. On the days that I sat there watching him, pretending to work, I wouldn't have been any more ashamed if I'd been spying for North Korea.

I never told Anna I'd gone to see him, though I did, via some of the most faux-casual, unconvincing conversational maneuvers I'd ever made use of, try to get her to tell me more about why they'd broken up. And I never spoke a word to him, except for once when he came over to ask if I was using the other chair at my table (I grunted something that we both understood to mean, *No, take it, leave me alone*).

Instead I went on seeing her at night, always denying that there was anything the matter, and I went on fixating on him, imagining the noises she made under him, thinking of the things she must have said to *him,* if she thought that my arms were strong. It seemed to me that for the first few months of our relationship (when had I started thinking of this as a relationship?) I'd somehow missed the most basic fact of all: I was just a placeholder, something to keep her occupied between the men she actually wanted to be with. The truth of it seemed mathematical and terrible. I could only love her so long as I could be tormented by her; and the more I was tormented, the more convinced I became that my love, which had started out as an absurdity, was the genuine article.

There is, I've noticed, a direct relationship between the handle I have on my life at any given moment and the handle I have on my email. On the laptop glowing in front of me while I strained to see Max's tattoos, my emails were multiplying like termites.

> Hi sweetie— Quick question about setting up the new speakers in the living room. Probably easier to show you in person. Any night this week you might be able to stop by?

> Hi Adam, I got your name from David Shapiro, who mentioned that you were potentially interested in UVA. I graduated last spring and now I'm clerking for a 2nd district judge and living pretty close to you in D.C. (I think). No pressure, but if you ever want to get together and chat about the pros and cons of your different options . . .

And from Thomas's mom:

Dear Adam, I just thought I'd try writing to you again,
since we ran into your mother the other day and heard all
about what you're up to. It sounds as if you're doing just
as wonderfully as you deserve. I'm sure your mother mentioned it, but Thomas continues to travel and continues
to drive Richard and me up the wall with worry. I know
you're very busy, but we'd love to catch up at some point,
if you ever find yourself with a free afternoon.

Responding to Sally—or even responding to one of the messages not from Sally—would have been as far beyond me as doing a cartwheel across the room.

Instead, when I did look at the computer, it was either to reread months-old emails from Claire ("dinner at 7:30 or 8?" "my boss is actually I think maybe mentally handicapped") or to do research into questions like: *What's the name of that actor with the cleft palate?*

Or, *Is Rosetta Stone really supposed to be good for learning Mandarin?*

Or, *Are there any good places for a solo traveler in South Dakota?*

Or, *How do you know if someone's going to break up with you?*

Or, *How do you work out your forearms?*

Or, and this one I could never actually formulate into a searchable question, so instead the thought just worked its way through me like the caffeine from all of those free refills of coffee, *Does it feel this way for everyone else?*

———————

When friendships start to die, there's a temptation, the same way there is with crops or civilizations, to appease the gods with sacrifices. That's sometimes how I think about what happened—Mira was the unlucky person on the rim of the volcano at the moment when Thomas and I needed a way to make our bad luck stop.

But that makes it sound deliberate, when of course deliberate is the one thing it wasn't. There's a part of me, though, the part that takes over when I'm falling asleep, say, or waiting for a plane to take off with my forehead against the window, where the distinction between deliberate and accidental seems about as formidable as rice paper. Anyway:

Our friendship, by the time we were a year into high school, was in definite trouble. Some of this may have had to do with my having made the baseball team, which had pulled me off toward upperclassmen, guys more like my half brother than like Thomas, who took me to parties and got me drunk and turned me, for a few hours a week at least, into exactly the sort of person Thomas couldn't stand. And some of this, or maybe just another way of looking at the same part of it, was that Thomas had started to become puritanical. It was one thing to spend a Friday night reading about the history of railroads when you were in eighth grade and the only wildness you were missing out on had to do with who'd kissed who at a dance; it took a much stranger, harder personality to keep on claiming that your greatest pleasure in life was talking philosophy with your dad when suddenly there were *actual* pleasures to be had: girls willing to do the kinds of things that until then we'd only been able to see between static bands on channel 153; alcohol, the getting and consuming (and occasional vomiting) of which was now as important a pathway in most of our lives as the getting and consuming of sunlight in the life of a plant.

Thomas wanted no part of any of this. I wondered, at the time, if this might be a kind of slow-motion tantrum he was throwing on account of no longer being, in any obvious or indisputable way, the smartest kid in the grade. Two or three other D.C. schools had merged with Dupont for high school, so now all of us who'd gone to middle school together were like small-town folk who move to the city; it turned out there were other best singers, other best athletes, other geniuses— maybe Thomas thought he needed to ratchet up his strangeness if he was going to hold on to any sort of perch in the grade's collective brain.

None of this means, of course, that I didn't still think of Thomas as my best friend. It was just that it felt more and more like a friendship between a healthy person and a person in a home for convalescents, and I had to be careful not to bring too much of the outside world's cheeriness and nuttiness in with me when I went to see him. Except that's not quite right, because I don't think Thomas thought of himself as missing out on anything, when I did make the mistake of referring to a party I'd gone to or a girl I'd hooked up with. In his mind maybe I was the one in the home for convalescents and he was the one who had to pretend not to notice how much I'd changed, how much I'd deteriorated since my good years.

One place, anyway, where all of this dropped away and we continued to be the same close, clever young men we'd always been was around the Pells' dinner table. With Sally and Richard we'd spend hours lost in the same kinds of intellectual/mystical seminar conversations that we always had, except I was more confident now than I had been when I'd first started spending time there—now I didn't hesitate to interrupt with whatever half-formed thought I had, and I didn't instantly go limping in the other direction if someone else at the table thought I was wrong.

"High school's really *agreeing* with you, huh?" Sally said to me one night. "If it were the olden days I'd say that your humours are well aligned. You seem happy."

And I was happy, most of the time. My mom and Frank seemed to have more or less accepted that they didn't need to bother me about whether I was going to be home for dinner or whether I wanted to go with them to see Yo-Yo Ma at the Kennedy Center. I'd lost some quality of nose-drip-having, food-in-my-braces-ness that had clung to me in middle school; puberty, although it of course entailed occasional voice cracks and pimples in the middle of my chin, felt for me like being a malnourished animal finally given a balanced diet. At last I could have my height measured by the nurse without feeling like I was going to have to apologize for something. I was starting to get used to things going well for me, the way a musician can sometimes fall into a rhythm where he knows that whatever note he plays, whatever riff he tries next, is just somehow going to sound right.

That summer, between ninth and tenth grade, I worked, which is to say volunteered, at a camp in D.C. for "underprivileged children" (the phrase, which I don't think struck me as weird at the time, came from the flyer in the Dupont guidance counselor's office). Just about everyone in the grade was either doing this sort of community service or a more extreme kind, where you'd go off to live in Vietnam or Ecuador for the summer and then come back with a deep tan and a commemorative string bracelet and a transformed perspective that would last until Thanksgiving. Thomas had an actual job, or a semi-actual job, helping a friend of his dad's with the research for a book on the history of the prison reform movement. A few times after a day at camp I took the Metro to meet Thomas at the Library of Congress. He'd be sitting behind a two-foot stack of books, filling notebooks with his tiny scribble. "Just wait maybe . . . twenty minutes? Then we can go back to my house, OK?" So I'd wander around the reading room with its sunless people lost in projects, wondering whether I should just go home.

Summer's a dangerous time for friendships—the whole predictable rhythm of the school year, with its drumroll of the week building, over and over, to the cymbal crash of Friday afternoon, is suspended; it's music with no time signature. Could I sleep over at the Pells' on a weekday now, since I didn't have to be at work until ten most mornings? His parents would have been fine with it, but no, probably not, since Thomas needed to be at the library as soon as it opened. Maybe just dinner then? But wasn't there something weirdly formal about that, as if I were an old college friend of Richard's, just passing through town?

Anyway, we usually ate with his parents and then, because their house never got cool in summer, even at night, we'd go walk through his neighborhood, either down along Connecticut or back in the direction of the woods, where we'd sometimes bump into other groups of kids our age drinking or one of Thomas's neighbors out throwing a tennis ball for his huffing dog. Most nights there were thunderstorms that were like indigestion in the sky, just a sort of redness and rumbling.

"I know I've been kind of the baddy," Thomas said one night. "One of my regimen goals this summer is to be more *fun*. I feel like I've let myself be cornered into being anti-fun. I feel like the reverend in *Footloose*."

My baseball friends were spending those same nights, we both knew, in a handful of guys' houses, drinking beer they'd bought with laughable fake IDs, smoking pot out of glass pipes, calling around to their cluster of girlfriends to find out where the party had happened to coalesce. So I—and this must have been what Thomas was responding to—had a slight feeling of babysitting as we walked soberly along together, using all our old phrases, making all our old jokes, not quite feeling all our old fondness.

The mischief we got up to at first, in the hopes of proving to both of us that we were still capable of fun, was fairly tame; we were like a long-married couple venturing nervously into a sex shop. We rang the doorbell at what was supposed to be Bob Woodward's house and then shouted, "*We are Deep Throat!*" as we sprinted off up the hill. We drank the red wine that his parents had left on the table and then pretended, him with much more excitement than me, not to be able to walk a straight line. We called the head of Dupont, Charles Gallant, and after planning to tell him we were from the IRS and that we knew how he'd *really* raised the money for the new gym, we hung up at the first sound of his Brahmin voice. I don't think either Thomas or I enjoyed any of these hijinks completely, but they were gestures, as I say; they were little ceremonies undertaken on behalf of something larger, like sullen Friday nights at temple.

I think now, although I've tried at various points to remember it otherwise, that I was the one who first proposed our taking the Pells' car out. We called this "committing grand theft auto," even though of course it entailed nothing more daring than waiting for Richard and Sally to fall asleep, then taking the keys from the basket by the front door. We knew, when we were doing it, that this was the most serious mischief we'd gotten up to—I could see Thomas getting nervous, and I could see him seeing that I was actually excited about this in a way I hadn't been about the prank calls or the doorbell-rings. This was when we'd just turned fifteen, so driving and everything to do with it, learner's permits and driver's ed and practice tests, had a kind of close-enough-to-touch electricity for us, or at least for me. My stepdad had, in the parking lot of his club, let me drive slow circles in his Lexus a few afternoons, so I didn't think of myself entirely as a beginner.

The Pells had an old black Volvo that they called "the Beast." We agreed that if we were caught taking it out, or if his parents somehow found out what we'd done, we'd say that I'd had a terrible headache and that I'd been in too much pain to walk so Thomas had thought he'd drive me just to the bottom of the hill, where we'd buy Advil. A ridiculous, nonsensical story, but one we figured no one could definitively disprove, and if his parents were the ones who caught us, we knew, although we wouldn't have said it, that the trouble we'd get in would probably only be of the you've-really-disappointed-me variety. It was hard to picture Sally and Richard much angrier than that; at worst Thomas and I could become like peers they disapproved of.

And anyway all we did, at first, was back the car out of the driveway with the headlights off, and then, once we'd pulled out into the road, drive a few houses down the hill toward Connecticut until we came to the yellow house with the perfect driveway for turning around. Then we'd go back up and pull in just the way we'd come (Thomas's nervousness about what we were doing came across mainly in how obsessive he was when it came to leaving the car in *precisely* the same place where we'd found it; he would lay out pebbles as markers for the tires).

I was, especially at first, usually the one who drove. We pretended we were a couple headed home from the office ("How was your day, sweetie?") or beatniks on the highway ("Unlock my window so I can get the breath of America in my hair!"). Of course everything to do with the car takes a much more prominent place in my memory now, but we probably did this a total of five or ten times over the course of the summer, always at around midnight, and with an increasing feeling of knowing what we were doing. Thomas once surprised me by stepping hard on the gas, so we seemed to lift off the road for about twenty feet, before he stomped on the brake and sent us straining against our seat belts. I experimented with slowly swerving, with driving up the street backward, with driving with my elbows on the steering wheel instead of my hands. His street turned out to be almost as dependably, boringly suburban as mine, despite being a few hundred feet from Connecticut: all the neighbors' houses were dark, and only once did we see anyone (a hurrying man with a cigarette) pass by on the sidewalk.

The transition, as I saw it afterward, came on a night (this would have been in July, because the Pells were just back from Maine) when I said that I wanted to act out a scene from *Terminator 2*. Thomas hadn't seen *Terminator 2*, of course, so I had to describe to him the part I meant: T-1000, with one arm transformed into some sort of bar or hook, leaps onto the windshield of the Terminator's car and hangs there, blocking his view, as the Terminator tries to shake him off. We would do this, I explained/argued, at all of three miles an hour, but still Thomas took some convincing. Finally he agreed, on the condition that if he so much as touched the horn I had to jump off to the side. So I lay there on the windshield a couple of feet from Thomas's concentrating face for what must have been twenty or thirty feet, hanging by my fingertips from the little rim by the roof, enjoying the weird sensation of the car creeping along under me. Then he tooted his horn and we were moving so slowly that I was able to hop off and land on both feet. Thomas tried it too (I started to do some of the subtlest possible swerving, not to shake him off but to imitate it, and he pounded the windshield with his fist). Nothing happened and no one saw us, and we put the car back in the driveway having spent another night feeling better about each other than if we'd just sat in his house waiting for Letterman to come on, complaining halfheartedly about my stepdad or about people at school.

But the jumping on the hood, I'm convinced, was what put the possibility in our minds—the trouble with mischief, like the trouble with drugs, is that you need more and more to feel what you felt before. So the next time we took out the car (and this was just after midnight on August 7, 1997, which for a long time glowed in my mind with a kind of black-light fluorescence), Thomas was driving and I was jogging along on the passenger's side with the idea that I was going to dive in through the open window: that was going to be the stunt. But Thomas must have had another idea, or he must have misunderstood me, because just as I was timing myself to make my jump, he unclicked his seat belt, opened his door, and leaped out with a flourish, like someone leaping from a canoe as it approached a waterfall. He tried to say afterward that he'd thought that the plan was for me to dive in through the window and take over the driving, but I didn't believe him; he would have known that a thing like that could never have worked, and even if it might have worked, it would have taken much better timing than we had. What I think happened is that he thought he was shifting the car into park when he was actually shifting it into neutral—he thought that for once, by leaping from a car he was driving, *he'd* be the one to take us both by surprise: see how impulsive and dumb he could be?

Well the car kept going. There was a moment when both of us stood there registering what was happening, in which all the sound seemed to go out of the world except for the paint-roller noise the tires made on the road: *Oh my fucking God, the car is still moving.* And if we hadn't stood there for that moment, if we'd saved our disbelief for afterward . . . But maybe it wouldn't have made a difference, because the moment was just a moment, and we caught up with the car well before the intersection. But by that time it was rolling a little faster, since this was where the hill got steeper, and the fucking passenger door was locked and I couldn't have, or wouldn't have, thought of diving in through the passenger window now, when there was a good chance that I'd just get stuck with my legs hanging out into the air and then where would we be? But why couldn't Thomas get his door open and get back into the driver's seat? Afterward he said the door handle stuck but I didn't and don't believe him: it was animal panic, it was fumbling, it was the kind of physical idiocy that was never far from the surface in him.

Connecticut Avenue, even at midnight on a Wednesday, is never completely empty. And on that particular stretch, where it intersected with Thomas's street, there wasn't a stoplight for a couple of hundred yards, so the cars tended to speed, as long as there weren't any cops around. So there's every reason to think the SUV was speeding as it approached Macomb. And, so long as I'm speculating, it seems likely that the woman crossing Connecticut, who'd been at a friend's house on Lowell and who was already halfway across the street, might not have looked for cars, since in the middle of the night walkers tended to be more reckless. These things, I think, aren't just possible but maybe even likely. Anyway, even if he hadn't been speeding, the man driving the SUV wouldn't have had time to decide what to do about the Volvo; it was black and the headlights were off; its nose would have appeared in his view and his hands would have turned the wheel before he'd even have had time to make a sound.

I'd never before—not when my mom had fainted in an elevator at Hecht's, not when I'd almost biked directly off a hiking trail into a ravine—felt horror anything like what I felt in that instant of hearing the scream of brakes and, half a heartbeat later, the scream of a woman.

There's a moment just after breaking something (the glass slips from your fingertips, your elbow catches the vase) in which it feels like if you stand there, absolutely still, baring your teeth, you should be able to suck time backward like an indrawn breath. Your hand hangs there in the air, your eyes fall shut, you're like someone playing a children's game with a whistle and a voice that shouts, "*Freeze!*"

I was still in that moment when Thomas, who'd been standing beside me, started down toward our car, which had rolled to a stop half a lane into Connecticut and was sitting there untouched (only now did I register that among the things I heard *hadn't* been the crunch of metal or glass). I must have walked some ways down the block too, although I don't remember deciding to move, because I remember seeing the back of the man who'd been driving the SUV; he was bald-headed and wearing a white shirt, kneeling in the road, facing away from us. I remember seeing that our car sat in a puddle of dark between streetlights. And I remember thinking: *The cops aren't here yet; no one's come out of their houses yet; this won't last.*

It was Thomas who slipped into the Volvo, quick as a mouse disappearing into a crack in the wall, and it was him who reversed, more smoothly than either of us had ever driven before: an indrawn breath. But it was me who ran after him, who guided the car into the driveway, who, trembling afterward in Thomas's bedroom, trying not to hear the faraway sirens, agreed: not a word, not a word, not a word.

Anna and I were lying together on the bath mat in their guest bathroom one afternoon that May. This bathroom had an enormous claw-foot tub, which we'd been in and were now outside of, listening as it slurpily drained, and I said, thinking I sounded so casual that it couldn't possibly be a problem, "What was that Max guy's last name again?"

"Is *that* what this is about?"

"What?"

"The way you're being. You're one of those jealous people! I told you!"

"One of what jealous people? I just couldn't remember if—"

"Jesus Christ, this is idiotic." She wrapped herself in a towel and left me lying on the floor, looking at the underside of the sink, my back stuck to cold porcelain, surrounded by the smell of blown-out candles.

We had one of our only bad fights that afternoon, storming around the house in our towels, unable to wave our arms. She said that if I was calling her a slut then I should just go ahead and say it, and I said that if she was looking for some dumb Texan fuck buddy then she should find somebody else, because that wasn't who—

"How do you know he's Texan?"

"You said."

"No, I didn't."

On most days my strategy was less direct, if not any more successful. I'd started doing push-ups (which required clearing a space on the floor of my room and waiting for Joel to leave for work in the morning, so he wouldn't ask me what I was doing). Whenever I sat around I squeezed a tennis ball, switching hands every couple of minutes. I tried, when Anna and I were together, to cultivate an air of . . . mysterious masculinity. Sensitive cowboy-hood. I let stubble grow on my cheeks. I carried her up the stairs and laid her on the bed as gently as if I were launching a raft. I let her know that I was thinking of spending a month this summer driving across the country alone.

I should never have tried. My appeal, what appeal I had, was of a different type—tousled and sandy haired and slightly soft around the edges. Women wanted to mother me, not be ravaged by me. I'd known that at various points, but in my state that spring I'd forgotten it. And so I was on a campaign to ravage; like a caveman assailant I dragged her to the floor in that gloomy front room. I lifted her up onto the workbench in the basement. And on the hot night in May when everything ended, I led her, kissing and shedding clothes and stumbling, directly from the front door where she met me to the kitchen in the back of the house, where, in only my socks, I swept aside a bagful of junk mail and laid her on the same small table where we'd sat drinking tea four months earlier.

In my defense, it was a Sunday, which was one of the nights that Peter had the boys, and it was eight o'clock, which meant that it was too dark outside for neighbors to see in. I'd thought about these things, which is probably an argument against my being the sort of person who should have his way with people on kitchen tables.

Anyway: *. . . yes . . . yes . . . oh my God, you're so . . . Oh my God, there . . . yes . . .*

There was often a point, when I was a teenager masturbating in my room, when I would think: *If someone were to walk in right this second I don't think I could stop.* The orgasm gravity was such that all considerations, even ones about not masturbating in front of my mom or Frank, were out the window. At the time I'd never had occasion to find out if this was really true.

It turns out it's never too late to stop, really. Gravity can be reversed in the time it takes to snap your fingers. Or in the time it takes to hear someone rap his knuckles against the glass in the kitchen door.

It was strange, in retrospect, how immediately I knew that the sound wasn't made by a squirrel or a branch or by anything other than someone watching us. Peter's face was about a quarter inch from the window (he had to hunch slightly to look in, and he held one hand like a visor to his forehead). Beside and behind him were the tops of two little brown-blond heads. Thomas used to think it was funny, when I fell asleep watching a movie, to wake me up by putting his face as close to mine as he could and waiting. This felt like that, if instead of Thomas's face waiting when I opened my eyes I found a lion's. Only because a chair was behind me did I not turn and race out of the room.

The *panic!* chemicals that were dumped into my blood-stream made everything seem fine-grained and slow. It seemed to take minutes for Anna to grab a dish towel from the faucet with which to (sort of) cover herself, minutes for her to unlock and open the door, minutes for Peter to enter and begin to shout, minutes for me to pick up the red oven mitt and settle on a way of holding it so as to minimize my exposure. My penis hung there dumb as a diving board. Luckily, if anything in this scene could be called lucky, Peter was so fixated on Anna, grabbing her by the arms and shaking her, that he seemed hardly to see me. And he'd apparently sent the boys (I could just hear the littlest bits of their voices) out to wait on the patio.

Peter and Anna were like two dogs that needed to be separated.

"*You selfish bitch—*"

"You motherfucker, come into my house—"

"*You slut, fucking this piece-of-shit tutor—*"

"Spying on me—"

"*You ought to be in jail—*"

"I hate you—"

"*You will never see the boys again—*"

"You just fucking try—"

"*Oh I will—*"

"You make me sick—"

At some point I realized that I was inching my way backward and that I was now practically in the kitchen doorway. Peter noticed it too. "And just what the fuck do you think you're doing?" he said, stepping toward me.

"I don't know."

"You don't have any fucking idea what I'm going to—"

I didn't know if he was going to stab me or tackle me or just keep walking toward me until he had me against the doorframe. So in one terrible butt-baring instant, I made a run for my pants and shirt (I'd have to do without my underwear) and, dressing as I fumbled with the door, bashing my shin on a bench, I escaped. I didn't look back to see if he was behind me, or if a butcher's knife was spinning toward me. I just wanted never to hear from or have anything to do with any of these people ever again. Close the door and change my phone number and change my name and be done.

Now I felt as if I were crazy. The street seemed so calm and springlike and ordinary as I limped down the steps that if my pants hadn't been unbuttoned, and if I hadn't been carrying my sneakers, I might have believed that none of it had really happened. I ducked into the coffee shop on Wisconsin where Anna and I had gone that first afternoon and hurried past the hostess to the bathroom, where I locked myself in and waited long enough—at least fifteen minutes, sitting on the toilet tank and dabbing at my face with wet paper towels—to be convinced that Peter wasn't out looking for me with a gun.

Here's what I learned, when I got home that night to an email from Anna:

Peter had come to drop the boys off because his mother had gone into the hospital after a dizzy spell. And he'd come to the back door because no one had answered at the front and because Anna had taken his keys. And he was planning on calling Barbara, my boss, to tell her that he was going to sue her and sue me and that every fucking parent in D.C. was going to know that her tutoring company . . .

And that Anna wasn't going to see me again. It was crazy and self-destructive, what she'd been doing, she said, and she needed to focus now on rebuilding her family. Luckily the boys hadn't seen anything, or hadn't understood anything they had seen, but it would be crazy to count on that kind of luck again.

I was too much in shock from the afternoon to know what I felt about anything, really. I wanted to write to Nicholas and tell him I was sorry I hadn't gotten to say good-bye. I wanted to confess my sins and become a monk.

The next day I got a message from Barbara that I could only stand to listen to the first few seconds of.

> Adam, I don't know where you are right now or what's going on, but you really need to call me, *really* need to call me, because I just had one of the most disturbing conversations of my life and I am freaking out because . . .

I spent the rest of that week in the apartment, in my bedroom, like Saddam Hussein in his spider hole. I gathered, from the quality of light in my one high window, that it was beautiful outside, but I had no real idea. Eventually I turned off my phone. I told Joel I was fine but I needed to be left alone for a while. Every couple of hours I worked myself into a panic that I was going to be in some kind of legal trouble, which would send me to the computer, where I'd lose myself in dozens of pages of useless, panic-worsening discussion threads about people with distantly related, or not at all related, problems.

On one of these afternoons I opened my computer and there was an email from Claire.

> Hey you. Is this totally awkward? I was all convinced that I definitely shouldn't write to you and that you might still be mad at me, or that I should be mad at you or something, but I'm kind of hoping all that's passed. Has it? I definitely feel on my end like there's been some kind of clearing up. Or maybe I just miss you? Or maybe the weather's just nice? Hard to say. But if you're still around and if you feel like getting a cup of coffee, consider me up for it.
>
> x,
> C

I understood that I'd been waiting for a note like this for a long time, that some important emotional buttons were being pushed, but for the moment the wiring in me all seemed to be disconnected. *Hard to say.* My adult life, which I'd thought I could build over the mess of my teenage life, had collapsed around me with a kind of beautiful speed. Sometimes I thought I was going to end up in jail, sometimes I thought I was going to end up driving into the Chesapeake Bay. My forearms were noticeably bigger. I couldn't remember the last time I'd had a glass of water.

Barbara sent me a letter on Capitol Tutoring letterhead telling me that I was in no way associated with the company, and that if I sought contact with Peter or Anna or any of the Raffertys, she was leaving open the possibility of legal action.

Claire sent me another email, this one saying she should never have reached out to me and that she wouldn't make that mistake again.

My mom called to say that they hadn't heard from me in ages and they were making flatbreads on the grill for dinner if I felt like coming by.

All of a sudden I had plenty of room in my life for thinking about Thomas. Room for thinking about everything.

I didn't sleep the night of the accident (one of the very few nights in my life about which I can say this unequivocally), and the next morning, under a sun like a bare bulb hanging just overhead, I had to walk down to Connecticut to get to the Metro to go to work. It was just after nine and it was already ninety degrees; throwing up seemed like a possibility that my body was just barely able to keep from becoming mandatory.

You'd think that coming upon the actual scene of the crash for the first time would have been momentous and horrible, but one effect of not sleeping is that everything starts to feel gauzy. Even if I'd slept eight sound hours on a feather bed, though, there might have been something dreamlike about it: hundreds of cars obliviously pushing their way toward work, sealed against the heat, getting honked at by buses.

Here was all the evidence I could see, in the few seconds I let myself slow down on the corner: an inside-out surgical glove in the gutter and a forked maroon trail in the middle of the road, about which my first thought was: *Isn't it weird that someone would have spilled something here that looks so much like blood?* Because you'd think that actual blood would have had to announce itself, it would have had to be cordoned off or cleaned up or at least somehow set apart from the flattened 7-Eleven cups and Lotto receipts. Otherwise what was to keep someone from mistaking it for raspberry syrup or for the kind of fake blood that comes in a white tube and that we used to squeeze onto the corners of our mouths before the Halloween parade? What was to keep a dog, like the German shepherd now walking past with its nose to the ground, from licking it up?

The worst of my suffering in those next few days—which felt like being poisoned, a freezing empty charge moving through me—came over me maybe once an hour, whether I was awake or asleep, helping to stack the nap mats at work or standing in the corner of my bedroom talking to Thomas on the phone. Each time I'd think: *I can't tolerate it, I'm going insane. This must be why people turn themselves in for things.* But then it would . . . not pass, exactly, but slip back into some more inner part of my nervous system, leaving me sore and shaken, and I'd think, *OK, I'll survive, it won't ever feel that bad again,* and I'd try to more or less go about my life until it happened again.

That the woman hadn't died was the thing I clung to, the fact I muttered thanks for when I was lying clammy in my bed at night, waiting to fall asleep. Thomas had had to hunt in the back pages of the *Post* for any mention of it (I'd pictured three-inch front-page headlines, global manhunts). We called what happened, when we talked about it, the "Occurrence at Owl Creek," and we both understood that he was going to have to be the one who monitored the news; within an hour of the accident I'd realized that he wasn't in as much danger of falling apart as I was, that his coldness or his detachment or whatever it was that made him him was going to be the vessel that got us through this.

The first story was on page A27:

PEDESTRIAN HIT BY CAR ON CONNECTICUT
A Cleveland Park woman is in critical condition at Sibley Memorial Hospital after being struck by a car

close to midnight on Thursday. Charles Lowe, 41,
was cited after his vehicle struck Mira Batra, 22, who
was attempting to cross Connecticut Avenue near
Macomb Street. Lt. Joseph La Porta of the Cleveland
Park Police said that alcohol was not a factor in the
accident.

So she hadn't died. So we weren't killers. These were like
rosary beads that I never let out of my sweaty hands. (And
finding out that she was twenty-two meant almost nothing to
me, or nothing more than any other age would have. Twenty-
two, when I was fifteen, seemed solidly adult.)

Another thing that kept me from collapsing completely
was the idea, which didn't seem quite so insane at the time,
that maybe our car hadn't had anything to do with the accident after all. Just a terrible coincidence. In middle school
we'd read a short story in our dreary blue English class anthol-
ogy called "The Necklace," about a woman who borrows a
diamond necklace from a rich friend for a party. She loses
it, then spends the rest of her life miserably trying to earn
enough money to buy a new one, only to find out on the last
page that it was a fake diamond in the first place. ("But it was
only a paste!" was the big, tragic reveal; the impact of this line
in class was undercut by Mrs. Fleche's monotone reading voice
and the fact that none of us knew what "paste" meant.) Anyway, I kept thinking, and trying to convince Thomas to think,
that we might be ruining our lives over something that really
hadn't been our fault: maybe the woman had been trying to
kill herself; maybe the man driving the SUV had been falling
asleep; maybe our car actually hadn't rolled so far out into the
road as it had seemed at the time. Who could really say?

*Driver says second car cause of Connecticut pedestrian accident;
police seek witnesses.*

When you're in a state of mind like I was for those couple
of weeks, everything you hear takes on terrifying undertones.
A few days after that second story ran we were eating dinner

at Thomas's when Sally said, "Admit it—were you out partying? You two look like you could just drop," and I couldn't answer right away because I couldn't breathe. Police cars cried, *A-dam, A-dam, A-dam.* I saw a man on the street with a bald head like the SUV driver's and the cable snapped on an elevator in my chest.

That Saturday morning we were driving with Thomas's dad to the Potomac to watch a regatta, pulling the same car into the same intersection, and Richard seemed to stop for a full minute before he turned onto Connecticut, as if the car were whispering to him. And in fact he did horribly say, not then but on the way back, "You know somebody got hit crossing right around here? You be careful when you're out walking around at night."

"We are," Thomas said. "Do we have any cream cheese at home?"

In one of the terrible dreams I had, starting that week and repeating for months afterward, I was standing in the middle of a highway knowing I was going to be run over and praying that the next car would be the one, that it would be done already.

"I don't understand how you're not more insane about this," I said one afternoon when Thomas and I were sitting on stumps in the homeless encampment, where we hadn't been for months. It was that part of the end of summer in D.C. when the gnats gather around your head, trying to be swallowed.

"I am, it's bad. It's really bad. But it's just us who know, literally just the two of us. So if we don't panic, I don't think anything's going to come of it."

"But how do you have a *choice* about whether to panic?"

"What do you want me to do? Bite my nails? Punch something?"

"I don't *want* you to do anything. But maybe you should acknowledge that because of you—"

"Because of us."

"Because of you! You! I would never have been so fucking stupid!" By that age I'd learned how not to cry, but only by putting my face and voice through contortions that were every bit as weird looking as crying.

But no matter how mad I got (and I did, in that conversation or another one, tell Thomas I hated him and that I was so sick of his fucking face that I never wanted to see him again), we were stuck together, closer, in a way, than we'd ever been before. My interactions with every other person in the world—the bizarrely sweet head counselor Carlotta at work; my mom, who would find me staring on the couch and ask if she could make me a sandwich; the homeless man who shivered all summer in his trench coat on the steps at the Friendship Heights Metro station—all of them took place on a stage, under lights, according to a script that couldn't have had any less to do with what I actually felt than if I'd been playing Mary Poppins. The only backstage I had was with Thomas. Only with him could I say, "This whole thing is really the fucking baddy," and feel that the pipeline between my brain and my mouth was finally, for a minute at least, open.

CLEVELAND PARK WOMAN, 22, DIES AFTER BEING HIT BY CAR ON CONNECTICUT.

When Thomas handed me the newspaper (we were sitting side by side on his bed, where we'd looked at *New Yorker* cartoons in seventh grade, where he'd shown me his drawings of Michelle Koller), I thought, for what turned out to be a last breath before going underwater, that this was about a different person. Connecticut was seriously dangerous for pedestrians, was the point, and it could always have been worse.

A Cleveland Park woman, Mira Batra, 22, has died after being struck by a car early on August 7. The cause, according to a spokesman for Sibley Memorial Hospital, was internal injuries sustained in the accident. The driver who struck her, Charles Lowe of Fairfax, has cited a second car as the cause of the acci-

dent. Police continue to investigate. Ms. Batra is survived by her parents, Manish and Amita Batra, also
of Cleveland Park, and her brother, Ajay Batra, 29,
of Baltimore. A memorial service is scheduled for
12:30 p.m. Saturday at the Hindu Temple of Greater
Washington, D.C.

"What do we do?" I said. I meant it on every scale: How
do we live our lives? How do we go back downstairs? How do
we survive the next minute?

Thomas shook his head, making a face I didn't recognize
right away that meant that he was crying; it was the kind
of crying, silent and painful looking, that can turn, with no
warning, into wailing. But instead of wailing he managed to
say, "*See? Happy now? Better if I fall apart?*"

I shook my head like a dog shaking water from its ears.

I wasn't, and I'm still not, the kind of person who knows
what to do when people cry (I've had more than one girlfriend
interrupt her tears to ask me why the hell I'm just sitting
there like a mannequin), but just then I didn't wonder at all: I
put a hand on Thomas's back and kept it there as he lay down,
kept it there as I lay down next to him, didn't say a word as his
breathing slowed down and as he finally, after what felt like
half an hour, started shuddering less and less. The newspaper
had fallen somewhere between the mattress and the wall. I
found myself staring at a birthmark on the back of his neck,
just above where my hand was, and every time I started to
panic I made myself notice one new thing about it (a whitish
hair, a pinprick red dot), and like that, vaguely comforted by
the thought that at least whatever was going to happen would
have to happen to both of us, I got through the hour.

"Thomas?" I said at one point, as if he might have somehow managed to die. "Thomas?" But he was, like a baby after
a bottle or a criminal after being caught, asleep.

———————

At some point in the spider-hole weeks after the Anna fiasco, I decided I couldn't live anymore with Joel. The darkness of my bedroom, the cereal bowls soaking in the sink, the mildewy towels hanging on the bathroom door—they weren't the cause of what had gone wrong in my life, but they were tangled up in it. So I called my mom one night ("I'd almost forgotten what you sound like!") and asked her to talk to Frank about whether any of his new apartments happened to be empty.

My stepdad, who'd made (and was continuing to make) more money as a lawyer than he had any idea what to do with, had bought a few apartments in a new condo in downtown Bethesda. He had the vague idea that he'd sell all but one, which he and my mom would move into when they retired, but I think he mostly just wanted something to talk about, to ask his secretary to make phone calls about, to keep track of now that they'd renovated every renovatable room in their current house. It's in the nature of empires to expand.

Adam, Mom tells me you're interested in apartment possibility. Give a call so we can discuss. Thanks. —F

As a stepfather Frank was uncomfortable (I remember once, when we were at the grocery store without my mom, that I reached up to tap his arm, and for a second, before he caught himself, he recoiled as if a stray dog had nosed him), but as a landlord he was a natural.

I moved in that weekend, and I realized, settling in that first night on my mattress on the floor, looking out over the empty brick courtyard with its Lululemon and artisanal gelato, that I was more alone than I'd ever been in my life. No girlfriend to know where I was. No roommate to stand in my doorway asking me to go out. Didn't Lee Harvey Oswald have an apartment like this? I came home at the end of each day (for rent I was organizing files at Frank's firm, sitting at the desk of a recently fired paralegal) and took the elevator to the ninth floor, where I'd lock my apartment door and proceed to make and break elaborate rules about when it was OK to start looking at porn and drinking.

I'd long since given in to both porn and drinking, and to the empty seasick feeling that came afterward, on the night when Sally wrote to me again.

From: <Sally Pell>
To: <Adam Sanecki>
Date: Fri, Jun 5, 2009 at 8:58 PM
Subject: old friend

Dear Adam,

I've been thinking about you since we ran into each other last month, and I keep thinking of things I should have said. In person I'm too polite, so I'm just going to be as honest as I can.

Adam, we're desperate. I'm not a writer like Richard, so I can't tell you how awful these past few months have been (and they've been even worse for Richard than for me). I don't know how much you know about what's going on, but we're losing Thomas, and if there's anything we can do to get him back, you can bet we're going to do it.

So I'm writing to ask a favor. ("Favor" doesn't sound right, but oh well.) I'm asking you to care. I know this must sound like some nagging teacher, and I'm sorry. But I know that for everyone there are people on the outside and there are people on the inside, and what I'm asking you to do, I guess, is to move Thomas in.

I don't know whether this means coming to see us or writing him a letter or even (God help me) going to look for him. But the first step is just to want to help him. I think you might be able to get through to him in a way that we can't anymore. I know it's all ancient history and probably very silly to you, but I think you still mean an awful lot to him. He never had another friend like you. I think he might still say you're his best friend, even now.

I'm rambling now. What I really want to make sure you know is just that your old friend, skinny Thomas Pell, is drowning. We all are, and we're reaching out to you for help. Let me know if you're willing to lend a hand.

Sally

Certain emails I read and then slam my laptop shut, as if I might be able to keep whatever news is in them from leaking out into my life. This was one of those, but none of my tricks—not shutting the computer, not even opening a new bottle of Cutty Sark—seemed to be working: the leak had already started. *We're reaching out to you for help.* A very bad idea, was all I could think. *Your old friend is drowning.* Well, so was I.

———

Remembering the accident, after spending a serious chunk of my life avoiding thinking about it, I've found myself wondering: So how did the guilt not kill me? How did I manage to go to class or apply to college or to worry about girls or to do anything, really, other than pay secret visits to Mira Batra's grave and weep?

And the only answer I can give myself, which might not make particular sense, is that I think it did wreck my life, but maybe only in the way that the collapse of an underground water-pipe system would wreck the life of a city. Which is to say: thoroughly but also, for a while at least, invisibly. So yes, I was back at school just a month after the accident, asking my history teacher smart-ass questions, playing with the new pitch speedometer the PE department had bought, and looking, to anyone who cared, like just the same ordinary, obnoxious fifteen-year-old I'd been on the last day of school the June before. But I was also having my first panic attacks (I woke up one night drenched and freezing, and when I was finally able to walk I went and took a Valium from my mom's medicine cabinet). For the first time in my life I was forgetting to eat. And sometimes in class, when I didn't even know I was feeling especially nervous, I'd look down and see that my leg was shaking, and the only thing I could do to control it was to press down on my thigh as hard as I could with the corner of a book. So, all was not OK.

One thing that was visibly different, once we were back at school, was that I couldn't be friends with Thomas anymore. I usually hate it when people say that they "couldn't" do things like that ("I just couldn't tell him," "I just couldn't leave the store without it"), but in this case I mean it physically: to keep going over to his house, talking to his parents, lying on the floor in his room, would have been like forcing myself to eat a human finger. I couldn't do it. I needed our fates, whatever they were, to be untangled.

It took Thomas a month or two to realize what was happening, and it may have taken me some time too. He'd stand waiting for me near the front steps where we usually met to walk to the bus stop and I'd wait inside, talking to baseball people in the lounge, until I'd see him leave. Or he'd call my house at night (I had my own line, so it only rang on the flat red-and-black phone in my room) and, after some number of tries, I'd just turn the ringer off. I did go over to his house a handful of times that fall, but I'd do everything I could to steer us away from talking about what had happened. I told him (I made sure, when we took walks now, that we walked up Macomb, away from Connecticut) about a girl named Ellen who I was starting to date. I had him explain to me in as much detail as he could what his mom's case against a real estate developer was about. Once in the middle of something I was saying about baseball (Thomas pretended, periodically, to be interested in learning what all the statistics meant), he said, "Just so you know, I looked her up the other day."

"Who?" I said. Inside me a hundred knives flew from their knife blocks. He ignored me.

"She went to Sidwell. Her parents live like five houses from Amy Crowley. Her brother's in med school at Hopkins."

"Why would I want to know this?"

"I think it's important. We can't just pretend that . . ."

I told him I absolutely could just pretend and, as soon as we were back in front of his house, I told him I had to go.

Another afternoon (it must have been the weekend, because his parents were home) we'd been up in his room and I went downstairs to pee, which meant walking past Richard's office. Richard usually spent his weekends at his desk, wearing reading glasses on the end of his nose, staring at his ancient gray computer. As I walked past I heard him say, "*Psst,* Adam, hey, come in here for a minute."

If robots ever become capable of meaningful communication with people, I think tone of voice, the density of information in it, is going to be one of the last things they master. I understood right away, by a kind of overheartiness, that Richard was embarrassed about whatever he was going to say to me, and, by the suddenness of how he called my name, that he'd been looking for an opportunity to have this conversation for a while. I also knew he didn't know anything about the accident—that would have been in his voice too—but still my legs went cold.

I sat down on the same corduroy armchair where I'd sat on a dozen other weekend afternoons getting help on English papers, under the white-framed window and the picture of Sally lifting baby Thomas onto a hay bale. On those English-paper afternoons Richard would sit reading, cross-legged, the tip of his pen hovering over the page, and I'd count rooftops through the window, feeling as if I were waiting for a wizard to cast a spell on me. Now he sat forward in his chair, his hands on his knees, and he'd just started to say "So" when he stood up to push the door shut.

"Do you think—there isn't, ah, any way I know not to feel a bit as if I'm accosting you here—but do you think there's anything *going on* with Thomas, from your vantage point? I know he's always going to present to Sally and me with the humble-scholar routine, but lately I'm getting something else, as a kind of bass line, maybe an angry vibe? Or shame?

I don't want you to feel under the Stasi's lamp here—if you'd rather not talk about it just say so and I'll go back to agonizing at my desk, which maybe I should have done from the beginning."

No, I said, I hadn't really noticed anything. Maybe it was just that there was more pressure now at school (as sophomores we'd started having monthly meetings with college counselors), or maybe it was just social stuff (by which I knew Richard would understand that I meant girlfriends and parties). As I was sitting there I thought: I've never lied to one of Thomas's parents like this before. It's so easy and so sad.

"I'd wondered how the whole ascetic thing was playing at school," Richard said. "And the trouble is I know where it comes from—you see old pictures of me and I've got this scowl, this kind of one-pointed, *I'm-much-too-serious-for-happiness* look, and now here it all comes again and I just don't know how somebody gets out of it except to grow up. Which seems OK until your kid's the one suffering. Well, he'll figure it out. Thanks for indulging me. And look, without getting too concerned-adult-putting-his-arm-around-you here, think about trying to convince him to come along to a party or something the next time you go. He's not as set in stone about all this as he thinks he is. He could really use you."

I walked out and back upstairs to Thomas's room, not quite believing that Richard was really sitting there in his office now thinking that everything would be better if only I invited Thomas to Roy Donnelly's next party. Sally called out good-bye to me that afternoon the way she always did (asking if I was sure I wouldn't stay for dinner, telling me to give my mom a hug), and I went along with it, singing my little part in our duet, standing in the doorway to the kitchen, but I just knew, as sure as if I'd been leaving for college the next day, that I wasn't going to be back.

And I wasn't, really (there may have been another time or two, but no more than that). First I stopped going over to the Pells' house, then I stopped looking for Thomas between classes, then I stopped saying hi to him in the halls completely. It was weird but it was also, once we were started on it, impossible to reverse; you can't go from ignoring someone to saying hi without some sort of conversation in between, some fight or explanation, but there was nothing I was willing to fight about, nothing I was willing to explain.

That summer Thomas worked again for the professor friend of his dad's; I went to a three-week baseball camp in Florida and spent the rest of my time going to the kinds of parties that I'd spent the summer before avoiding. At some point junior year Thomas seemed to accept that we weren't friends anymore. A couple of times, on parent-teacher nights or at awards assemblies, I'd see either Sally or Richard, and Richard would just give me a tight smile, but Sally would say, "You just *have* to come see us. We miss you!" But everyone understood, or seemed to think they understood: best friendships ended all the time.

My mom said to me sometimes (it was one of her handful of subjects, along with whether I thought it would be fun to go on a beach vacation once I graduated) that she'd always thought Thomas and I were a strange pair. And, she said, even though she never would have wanted to say it before, she always got the feeling that the Pells thought they were better than everyone else. Did I know (yes, I did) that she'd once left Sally a message asking if they'd come over for dinner and she had never even called her *back*? Oh well, she said. I'm sure he'll go on and get very good grades somewhere.

At the end of our senior year there was a class dinner out on the soccer field with caterers and round tables and a white tent; all the guys wore jackets and all the girls wore dresses and had their hair done up like ribbons (the end of senior year at Dupont is like the grand finale at a fireworks show: a dozen overlapping ceremonies and honors and farewells). By that time in the school year pretty much all the barriers between teachers and students have broken down; teachers let us call them by their first names, and they'd spend their class periods leading dreamy, what-does-it-all-mean discussions about how even though this particular group would never reassemble, we'd always have this shared experience to look back on, etc.

By bad luck, or by some parent-teacher committee's bad planning, Thomas and I were seated at the same table. We were a couple of chairs apart, and I spent most of the dinner talking intently to Philip Shailes on my left, who was the most boring person in our class, and who was telling me how he was planning to buy all his lamps and blankets at Bed Bath & Beyond now because they always jacked up the prices in August.

This was the kind of dinner where people drift away from the table as soon as the food is done to sit with their actual friends or to have heartfelt conversations with people they'll never see again. So there were a couple of minutes after the last of our table-mates had stood up, when Thomas and I were left alone. We looked at each other like a deer and a hunter, but I'm not sure who was who. Looking directly at him for the first time in a while, I could see that his skin was less delicate than it had been; now there was stubble on his chin and above his lip. He wore a light blue shirt and black pants that Sally must have bought him for graduation. "So," he said, "how're the wife and kids?"

"Oh, good, good. Yours?"

"Can't complain, can't complain. Actually," he said, breaking into his normal voice, "can complain pretty easily."

I nodded.

Thomas and I, who'd seen each other naked in the aquatic center locker room, who'd woken up a hundred times on side-by-side mattresses, who shared a secret more serious than any married couple . . . now we were awkward together. Awkwardness is like crabgrass: leave anything, anything at all, untended for long enough and it will grow until you can't see the concrete underneath.

"I heard you got into Penn," he said.

"Yup. You're going to Columbia?"

"Yup. Maybe you'll come to New York some weekend."

I nodded and shrugged.

"This has really been the Arc of all Arc de Triomphes, huh?" he said.

I nodded and did something with my face that looked like a smile but that said: *Don't try it, we're done, it's too late.*

He leaned away from the table in a way that meant he was about to stand up, but before he did he pulled a pen out of his pocket (one of the same blue pens that Richard always used on my English papers) and, on the bottom edge of my "A Banquet Under the Stars" program, he wrote two things:

Gut-bomb (which is what we'd used to sometimes say instead of good-bye); and, underneath that, in smaller writing: *Remember Owl Creek.* And then (did he smirk?) he was up and out of the tent, off to the bathroom to congratulate himself on having gotten through to me.

And he had, for a few minutes at least. I felt like I'd swallowed the point of his pen.

Sometimes as an adult I'll see one of those garbage trucks that they send out for special pickups, the ones with giant compactors built into their backs; they go around grabbing and crushing things like couches and car bumpers and wooden banisters, little landfills on wheels. And I always think, when I'm watching one work its way down the street, *No way, not that, it couldn't just swallow that,* but then it does, gulping down the refrigerator or whatever with just a little pause, and then off it goes.

There would have been about a dozen points, if you'd come to me when I was twelve, when I'd just arrived at Dupont with my green braces and my Redskins hat, and told me all the things that would happen over the next few years, when I would have said, *No, I won't be able to handle that. Sorry, I'll have to die.* But I could handle it, as it turned out, or I could live with it, or anyway I could live with it so far.

I tore off the bottom strip of my program, ripped the strip into confetti, and dropped the confetti into my water glass, and, before I got up to check if all the cake was gone, I dumped the whole mess in the grass under my chair.

I did finally write to Thomas, not the night of Sally's email but the one after. There are limits, it turns out, to how much guilt even I can cart around.

From: <Adam Sanecki>
To: <Thomas Pell>
Date: Sat, Jun 6, 2009 at 11:14 PM
Subject: ahoy-hoy

> Hey. It's been much too long, and I just wanted to see what you're up to. Things have been the baddy with me (girl stuff, job stuff), but I just moved into a new place and now I'm trying to figure out what to do next. Write back if you get a chance. I go pretty much whole days without talking to anybody other than the front-desk guy at work. With superlative gut-bombs, Adam

His response came at four in the morning my time, which I didn't have the brainpower to translate into India time. I was on my way to the bathroom, standing in my boxers, not at all sure that I wasn't still asleep.

From: <Thomas Pell>
To: <Adam Sanecki>
Date: Sun, Jun 7, 2009 at 3:58 AM
Subject: re: ahoy-hoy

> You ask what I'm up to but I know this question isn't
> yours, I have an image of a hired hand waving a treat in
> front of an animal's burrow. Know that I do not need trap-
> ping or rescuing (interchangeable) whatever S or R have
> said, I am not happy but I am not unhappy, I am where I
> should be. I know you can wash guilt from your face like
> dried mud, I can't, S and R know about Owl Creek, they
> won't admit it, I write to you rather than them because I
> know you understand, you suffer, and most important,
> whatever you pretend, you remember.

For the next couple of hours I lay in bed wondering how
you knew if you were having a heart attack. And the next
night, after a sleepwalking day at work, I wrote to Thomas
again, and again he wrote back at four in the morning. He'd
been in India for just over a year, but he wouldn't, or couldn't,
explain what he'd been doing there, except occasionally to
ramble like someone dictating with a high fever. Mostly
he just wanted to talk about his past, particularly the parts
related to our friendship and to the accident, as if he were fact-
checking an encyclopedia.

Over the next few weeks, even if it probably wasn't what
Sally had in mind, I don't think you could have said that I
didn't care. I was having my highway dream again, only now
instead of praying to be run over I was praying not to be.
Thomas and I were writing emails, sometimes three or four
a day, that were as strange and as personal as any interaction
we'd had since we'd exchanged boxers in eighth grade, for
solidarity.

As the summer wore on, I figured that this might be the
extent of it; that I'd keep writing to Thomas and keep talking

to his parents and keep lying in my apartment at night thinking about being fifteen, and in this way I'd pay my debts.
Wrong. At the beginning of July, Thomas wrote to his parents to say that if they didn't stop trying to get him home,
they'd never hear from him again. Around the same time he
stopped responding to my emails, and at first, despite Richard and Sally's mounting panic, I felt relief. He'd moved on
to some other obsession, I figured, some other long-lost correspondent, and I'd be free to resume my life in the present.
But after a week or two, by which time I'd begun to drift back
toward pretending he didn't exist, another email came from
him, just one line long:

> I've found the Batras, I'm getting ready, when it's time I
> will do what needs to be done, what's needed to be done,
> I'm sorry.

Right then I decided, or maybe I should say I realized
that it had been decided; it didn't seem to originate with
me. I didn't write back. Instead I spent a couple of hot gray
afternoons shuttling along Massachusetts Avenue between
the Indian embassy and my doctor's office, getting my tourist visa and my typhoid shot. Then on July 26, with my old
camp backpack stuffed in the overhead bin, I ate dinner in an
upright and locked position two miles above Maine. I slept
for a few hours and woke up in white sunlight to a breakfast
of microwaved rolls and freezing fruit. My left leg was completely asleep. My malaria medicine, or something, was making me feel dry mouthed and edgy. The cartoon airplane
ticking across the ocean on the monitor in front of me showed
us 2,063 miles from New Delhi.

· *Two* ·

As the taxi, which was really a kind of windowless van, carried me and my bag through the much-darker-than-America night, I kept having to fight down the impulse to tell my driver to turn around. It was just after nine, apparently, but my sense of time had gotten multiply exposed; I couldn't count the meals I'd eaten or sunsets I'd seen or Ambiens I'd taken since leaving home. Every couple of minutes I was having the same embarrassingly stupid thought, which was: Everyone here is Indian. The soldiers standing by the doorways with machine guns; the eight-year-old boys clamoring to shine my shoes; the women arranging candies and wind-up toys on bedsheets.

The right side of the highway was being constructed at that very minute by men standing on hills of steaming asphalt, which meant that the left side was clotted with trucks and bikes and rickshaws and little golf-cart-ish things like green-painted Flintstones cars, each with a horn blaring at a slightly different pitch. A few times my driver, a sweating, frowning bald man, had to swerve around dogs standing in stupors in the middle of the road like zombies in a video game. Also like a video game: we kept passing the same two billboards—a full-lipped woman in red laughing while she held a cell phone to her ear, and a wavy-haired soccer player kicking a ball straight out of a TV. WELCOME TO "THE BEST" HI-DEF!

We were going to Thomas's apartment, or anyway to an apartment where he'd lived at some point recently. The neighborhood was called Paharganj. Everything else I knew about where Thomas might have been could have fit on an index card (in fact it fit on the first few lines in the black-and-white notebook in my carry-on). I'd expected Thomas's parents to be brimming with leads and notions, but they'd proved surprisingly hopeless. Or maybe just fatalistic, after years of trying and failing to understand what their son was doing. A couple of weeks earlier, just after I'd agreed to go, I'd spent an awkward evening perched on the edge of their couch, feeling like I was being bid farewell before shipping off to war. At one point Sally had handed me a semirecent photograph of Thomas; he had long hair pulled back and a wispy beard, and he was smiling in a way that suggested drunkenness or maybe just the effects of whatever pills he was on. I held it with two hands, not sure how long I needed to stare before I could tuck it into my bag. "Your mission, should you choose to accept it," Richard said, seeming to sense that we'd slipped into a moment out of *Saving Private Ryan*.

For the past couple of weeks, Richard and Sally had been writing me emails; first just practical—addresses and phone numbers—then more and more a kind of journal of what they'd been through these past few years—things they couldn't say to Thomas, maybe, or things they'd tell anyone who'd listen. I hadn't felt so wrapped up in the Pells, so close to the daily workings of their lives, since I was fourteen.

Anyway, with each turn the road narrowed by a couple of lanes, until we were in a grim, dusty neighborhood where dogs slept on top of cars and the buildings seemed to be made of cinder block. The Pells had said that Thomas might have fallen in with some spiritual-burnout types, and this looked like the right place for it.

Decoding the building's buzzers, a plate-sized grid of silver nubbins, was just at the edge of my mental capacity. A barefoot, elfin man named Rory met me at the top of three flights of stairs; he wore loose cotton pants and stood looking recently asleep, with a slight smile and eyes just barely open. We'd talked once when I was still in D.C., and he'd seemed bizarrely unfazed that I was hoping to come stay in his apartment while I looked for a lost friend. "No worries, no worries." He'd never actually met Thomas (he'd only been in Delhi since May), but he knew people who knew him, and he said they had a spare bed. He was, I saw now, a man with the metabolism of an iguana; he wouldn't be fazed by the explosion of the sun. He took my bag and shuffled ahead of me into an apartment that felt like it had once been a locker room. It was dim the way fluorescent-lit rooms are dim, with a color-flecked cement floor and a half-dozen wooden partitions. There were collapsed, filthy couches, lamps set on top of plastic crates, a strip of speckled flypaper hanging in the corner. There was a cloying, oily smell in the air coming from a candle burning on a trunk.

"Your bed's that one. Sheets are in that stack."

The word *bed* was like a glimpse of water in the desert, but before I could sleep Rory took me up onto the roof. One of the girls who was over had lived there when Thomas had, Rory said. The night sky was like a sagging yellow tent ceiling. From the street I could hear firecrackers and frantic techno-ish music. The forecast on the plane had said "Smoky heat," which I'd assumed was a mistranslation, but the air actually was both smoky and hot; since the second we'd landed I'd been smelling burning tires, which probably explained my stinging eyes and running nose. In the half-dark of the rooftop I got an impression of a scene like a concert lawn: candles and devil sticks and skunky pot.

I think travel must have made more sense, psychologically, in the era of ocean voyages; in the three months it took to get from America to India you would've realized the extremity of what you were doing; you would have stepped off the boat knowing exactly how far you were from your old life. But I, sitting in a plastic lawn chair on that rooftop, gazing out through the smog at what seemed to be the dome of a mosque, still had a receipt from the Bethesda Row CVS in the front pocket of my jeans.

A group of people was sitting around a beach towel, playing a game that involved pressing a card against your forehead. There was a brutish barefoot guy with a shaved head. A forest-sprite girl leaning against the brute's knee. A dreadlocked smirking guy who kept doing something double-jointed with his wrists.

"—I think I've got to fold again, fuck."

"—maybe that's exactly why she can't, you know?"

"—I guess I just can't see how that's not just another kind of decision . . ."

"Hey, so you're Thomas's friend?"

It took me a couple of seconds to register that someone was talking to me. It was an Earth Mother–ish girl with a nose stud and a yellow bandanna, pulling a Kingfisher from the water in the cooler I hadn't noticed I was sitting next to. "You went to high school with him, right?" Her name was Cecilia, and she was from a town in Minnesota where people just didn't, she was eager to have me understand, go to India. She made me remember for the first time in years a hippie camp counselor I'd once had, the first woman I'd ever seen with armpit hair, belter of Sly and the Family Stone in the camp van. Cecilia had moved to Delhi a couple of years ago to study "bodywork," and now she was taking, or maybe teaching, a course in conflict resolution.

"I've been worried about Thomas. Have you talked to him since his solo?"

"Hmm?"

"He was supposed to be back for a session with Guruji almost a month ago. Somebody said they saw him a couple of weeks ago at the cremation grounds." While she talked she kept adjusting her neck, like a pigeon.

"And where was he supposed to be?"

"He was on his precept retreats. He was just about to do the cave."

The forest sprite came bubbling up, dragging the brute along behind her ("What's up?! Did you just get here?"), and Cecilia melted off toward the card game. The sprite, Nicola, looked vaguely South American and had eyes that made her seem permanently surprised. Another obvious thought I kept finding myself having: There are so, so many people in the world.

I stayed up on the roof for another half hour or so, drifting in and out of conversations, being introduced and introduced again, telling people how I knew Thomas, saying yes I'd be sure to do that, no I'd make sure to avoid doing the other, hearing the word *guruji,* sometimes the name Sri Prabhakara, like a recurrent scrap of melody.

"So he's a meditation teacher?"

"Mmm . . . I would say more a philosopher." (This was Nicola's brutish boyfriend, Rik, who turned out to be somber and Danish, and to have spent the past couple of years playing semiprofessional basketball in Japan.)

"And is he old?"

"Seventy-five? Eighty? It's not obvious to look at him."

There was a nervous excitement that fluttered around any mention of Guruji, as if he were a movie star someone heard might be eating in the back room. Everybody who'd ever lived in the apartment knew him, apparently; it was a kind of study-house. I found myself picturing an old man with clouded-over eyes, a long beard, fingernails grown into rams' horns; a cross between Ben Gunn and Gandhi.

"I didn't actually see it," the dreadlocked kid said to me, tilting his head back to finish a beer, "but somebody rode past your friend meditating by the train tracks like way the hell out. I think maybe he's like a . . . dharma ghost." This could be one of the frat houses at Penn, I kept thinking. But instead of talking about who was bringing Jägermeister and who was having sex, they were talking about compassion retreats and private sessions with Guruji. I was standing by the railing listening to an intense Israeli man named Jonah tell me about *hijras,* a caste of Indian transvestites who apparently have the power to curse people, when I realized I was sleeping with my eyes open.

I'm going to need to expand my vocabulary when it comes to the varieties of bad sleep, the way someone on an ocean voyage would need to distinguish between types of storms. That first night in Thomas's old apartment, anyway, was a collision of various fronts: nervousness, heat, jet lag, digestive unrest. My bed turned out to be a green canvas cot, wedged onto the floor behind a partition. The conversation of the people on the roof came directly down to me as if they were shouting through a pipe; every time the techno music seemed to have stopped it would turn out just to have paused to gather its strength. I kept being woken up by something tickling my forehead and gusts of black-smelling mold. By two a.m. I'd decided that unbeknownst to me, India, like Iceland, must have a season of sunless days, and at three I took a sleeping pill and then had a dream about choking on chalk dust.

Apparently at some point in the last aching stretch before dawn I got out my notebook, because when I woke up it was open on my pillow, with a new line at the bottom of the first page in handwriting I almost didn't recognize as mine:

shouldn't have come. check flights. to find him would be a literal miracle, something to teach in schools, a moon landing.

From: <Thomas Pell>
To: <Adam Sanecki>
Date: Mon, Jun 15, 2009 at 4:43 AM
Subject: re: (no subject)

. . . You mention guilt but I would say that for years,
despite reason to be, I was not a guilty person, my mind
ran along other tracks, sophomore year, junior year,
it started, I would lie in my room at Columbia, ninety-
eight-square-foot cell, remembering everything, not the
crash, but other things, older, I would dream of my toad
Lewis whom I killed or thought I killed at seven years old,
before you knew me. He was loathsome to me, physically
repellent, he ate mice and crickets, they puffed their bag
with jumping, I used to imagine him dead, I would think
of birds coming through the window and carrying him
away, one morning I came downstairs to feed him, I was
devout, the glass of his case was hot, the dial had been
turned to High, he was a briquette, his eyes were dried
currants. When I called to S and R they came downstairs,
bathrobes and bare feet, said, Oh no Rosabelle must have

done it cleaning up, or one of them must have brushed against it, they wanted to absolve me, but I knew I had, I had no memory of it but I knew with my wishing, it had to be. I wept in my room that night, S came in, not understanding, she sat with me, said, Yes, it was so sad, he had been such a wonderful toad, hadn't he, she was sure he hadn't suffered, it had happened while he was asleep, we'd get another. I was not good, I was not well, terrible things happened when I wasn't careful, this may have been the first time I understood it.

From: <Richard C. Pell>
To: <Adam Sanecki>
Date: Tue, Jul 7, 2009 at 10:02 PM
Subject: re: greetings

. . . My worry started to tick—parental Geiger counter—
sometime his junior year, when phone calls started to
have an edge of hastiness, partial accounting. Classes?
Fine. Dorm? Fine. Roommate? Fine. He was staking out
mental residence elsewhere.

All this, keep in mind, had 9/11 in the background—it had
only been a year, so still very much in the penumbra of
everything changed. If anything was going on with him,
we thought it might be that—going to school a few miles
uptown from Ground Zero, we'd assumed some of the
atmospheric panic—Cipro and Wolf Blitzer touch-screen
maps of Afghan caves—might have seeped in. He'd
started kind of fear-blurting—should he ride the subway?
Get a gas mask? So we probably misread the signs. A

nervous breakdown after 9/11 was like a lost voice in a Trappist monastery.

Thanksgiving was another worry-tick—I remember mostly o'er-leaping talk, clattering plates, and Thomas at the center, wax figure in a gallery. This was his vegetarian debut, so a part of me thought, OK, projecting holiness, making clear he's not a party to the feast, got it. (In college, my meatless years, I sat at my parents' table in front of a plate of bacon, fingers of enticement beckoning like cartoon pies on a ledge.) But he was establishing the mental territory.

Then a few months later the phone rang too late on a Sunday night, a girl from Columbia—she'd just talked to Thomas and she was scared. He'd told her he was very sick—brain tumor, months to live, she's the only one who can know. My first thought was: shrapnel from a romantic blowup. Thomas, at that point, was very much a novice, so I was thinking, OK, he falls for a girl, nothing doing, he comes up with this story to try to get her attention. Somewhere between a protester setting himself on fire and John Cusack with his boom box: you have no choice but to feel for me.

But when we talked to Thomas, he sounded—sweaty. Upset to hear she'd called us, panicky about what we knew, what we weren't saying. Asking me if he was going to have to go to war—this was just before Iraq, fear becoming anger in the national forebrain. I started thinking drugs. Some party where he gave in, tired of protecting the prize intelligence.

Day or two later we got a call from the dean. Thomas is missing class, blowing off his adviser. Flunking three out of four courses. OK. And oh, by the way, if he doesn't shape up we're going to need to ask him to take a semester off and make up credits elsewhere. Lion pride. Right.

So we drove up to New York, not getting anywhere on the phone. Both of us took off work, five hours up I-95, into the dorm, still half expecting the whole scene to dissolve into misunderstanding. The dorm, by the way, felt like a playroom: hallway of pajama-wearing girls lying on the floor trailing phone cords, boys bouncing lacrosse balls off concrete walls. Leaders of tomorrow.

We knocked—THOMAS PELL in bubble letters still from the RA—and he finally opened the door and the smell was . . . shocking, but not in any familiar collegiate way. Sinister. Rotting greens, decay. I found myself thinking, unbidden: This is the smell of a crazy person's room.

And he was very much confused, embarrassed, over-whelmed. Skinnier than we'd ever seen him, dirty, this kind of pubic beard, still talking about being sick, about war. The room was a mess but almost sculptural, sheets wadded up on the windowsills, fans on chairs. He wanted to know—staring straight ahead—whether he had cancer, said he knew we'd been talking to doctors. He was on his bed, wrapped in sheets, the phone was next to his pillow, there was a cup of what smelled like piss. Sally was trying to pull him to his feet, crying, take the measure of him, I was kind of . . . feeling for the seam, like when he used to have night terrors: OK, where's the awareness in there. Nothing doing. So I just hugged him—OK, we'll get through this, you're OK. Trusting that this, surprise of the dorm visit, had to be the worst moment. Except in the hug I realized two things—one, the smell, the worst of it, was his body, and two, the weight he'd lost. Imagine hug-ging an empty sleeping bag. For me that was the genre change, drama into horror, spring 2003—that hug with the body that was and wasn't Thomas.

So: Sri Prabhakara. Here, from what I was able to gather during my first semiconscious couple of days, was the story. I heard some of this from the Earth Mother, Cecilia, who met me for lunch at a nightclub-feeling Mexican restaurant near her school, and some of it from people Cecilia introduced me to who'd vaguely known Thomas.

Apparently, until some point that spring, Thomas had been living on his own in Delhi. No one, or at least no one I talked to, had any idea where. Maybe he'd been homeless (there were groups of expats who lived with their wormy dogs and guitars outside the bus station at Kashmiri Gate), maybe he'd just been living in another apartment. Almost certainly he hadn't been working for any sort of education company, the way he'd told his parents he was; by the time people in the study-apartment had started to see him he had long hair and sun-chapped skin, and he was wearing clothes that looked like they'd been pieced together from a children's giveaway bin.

People occasionally saw him at the outdoor bazaar in Paharganj (goats wandering down the middle of the street, bearded men huddling over hookahs in doorways); the bazaar was on the way to Sri Prabhakara's center. Thomas would be muttering and handing out fennel candies to kids, or he'd be washing himself in a runoff pipe at the end of the alley. To each other, they called him Skeletor. Maybe this was his prime looking-for-the-Batras period, maybe this was pure fugue and craziness.

Anyway, after a few weeks of not having seen Skeletor, a couple of Guruji's students took a different way to the center one night and came across him in terrible shape: barefoot, filthy, sprawled on the steps of a temple. At first one of them mistook him for a dead body. You could have scooped him up with a shovel and tossed him like a bag of empty cans. One of them went up and tapped his shoulder, and he bolted upright. "Fine, fine," he said, when they asked if he was all right. "Good, just a little tired, was I asleep? I think I fell asleep. I'm sorry, I'm sorry."

They convinced him to come along with them to the center. They made him eat rice and drink a bottle of Thums Up, then wadded up some paper towels and helped him wash the dried blood from his ear. After Guruji's talk they took him home to the *barsati,* and once he'd showered (they said he left a ring of orange around the drain, still not entirely gone), he slept the night without sheets, at his own insistence, on a corner of the roof. He answered questions about what he'd been doing as if he were talking about a dream. *I was looking for someone. I had a fever. It wouldn't stop raining.* As far as they could tell he didn't own anything except the clothes he was wearing and a kid's backpack in which he kept a rubber-banded wad of money and a camping Thermos. They asked the next day if he wanted to stay for a while and he murmured, Yes, thank you, OK.

Except for the rice that first night, all he ever seemed to eat were the little paper bowls of lentil mush the Hindu temple ladled out once a day in Shiva Mandir, but he was coming back to life. A splotchy red wound/rash he'd had on his neck and shoulder was clearing. His eyes were getting brighter. They finally started getting bits of a slightly more coherent story out of him: from D.C.; in India for six months; looking for an old friend; sleeping outside because he didn't like being alone.

Mostly he listened. He could be kind of scarily attentive, actually, sipping tea from his Thermos, staring. He started sitting in on the post-dinner meditations sometimes, folded and still on a cushion in the corner of the room. He became like the apartment's mascot, an actual wanderer whose strangeness lit up the rest of them. When he wasn't meditating, he was either staring out the front window, trying to feed pieces of Ready Brek to the little black birds, or typing furiously on other people's computers (he was always appearing next to your partition and asking, in a voice so quiet you almost couldn't hear it, if he could borrow yours).

He started going to Guruji's Sunday-evening discourses, sometimes staying at the center all night afterward. He walked barefoot through the market where he'd almost died, patting children and goats on the head, chewing salty-sticky squash seeds that you could buy wrapped in newspaper for five rupees. Every June Guruji gave a six-week series of introductions to the practice, and this happened to be when Thomas had come into the picture.

Practice? Discourses? At this point, the people I was talking to became hard to pin down. Not, I didn't think, out of any sense of secrecy; it was more just the weirdness of explaining to an outsider something absolutely fundamental. *See, there's this thing humans do every night where they lie down and close their eyes and just sort of wait for strange visions to come . . .*

Anyway, here's what I got: Sri Prabhakara was a spiritual mini-celebrity who'd somehow cultivated, over the past couple of decades, a group of foreigners who bought his pamphlet-looking books, listened to his crappily recorded talks, and, if they were especially devoted, flew to Delhi and spent a few months living in one of the *barsati* apartments near his center. Once they were there they'd go on retreats and take classes on his precepts and do the sort of work (scrubbing toilets, sweeping stairs) that interns and cult members are best at. Guruji was uneducated, a former shopkeeper, and he wasn't associated with any particular religion or group; he was an all-purpose expert in suffering, the self, the veils beyond the veils, etc. When he was young he'd been taught by Sri Something-or-Other, who'd been taught by an even holier Sri Something-or-Other, and so on and so on back to the beginning of time.

Thomas had apparently revealed himself, over the course of those six weeks, as being especially adept (is it weird that I felt a flicker of jealousy at first hearing this?). Guruji had taken an interest in him from the first time they'd talked, and by the end of June (when we were exchanging emails and I was doing data entry not much more interesting than toilet scrubbing), Thomas was meditating more than anyone in the apartment. He'd spend whole days cross-legged on his corner of the roof, or walking slow lines back and forth along the railing. At some point he'd shaved his head; he'd memorized the precepts; he'd tied the red string around his wrist that was the symbol for having given yourself over to the practice. And after just a couple of months—less time than anyone had ever heard of it taking—Guruji had declared Thomas ready for the retreats that were, apparently, something like final exams. First a day alone in the center (the center, which I walked past on my second night, looked like a low-on-funding public library). Then a couple of days of fasting in the forest. Then another couple of days of walking along the bank of the Yamuna while contemplating death. Then finally, if each of those had gone well (not the usual course of events, apparently), a week in a cave in the Kumaon Hills, where Sri Prabhakara and the various Sris before him had all achieved their enlightenments.

Thomas still wasn't anything like normal looking by the time he started on his retreats; if you'd passed him on the street you would have thought he was homeless and/or starving. But compared to how he'd looked before, he could have been in *Men's Health*. He must have gained ten or fifteen pounds since moving into the *barsati,* and he'd taken to wearing a pair of baby-blue pajamas that one of the girls had lent him, so at least his clothes weren't rags. He did the day at the center, the nights in the forest, and the walk by the river all without a problem, but then in July, just when he was about to go off to the cave (he'd been training himself for the dark by sitting between retreats in the supply closet), he'd disappeared.

Weren't they worried that he'd died? That he'd maybe tripped on a rock going into the cave and bled to death at the foot of some godforsaken Indian mountain? No, apparently he'd never left Delhi at all. A couple of people knew people who said they'd seen him since then, back in the Paharganj bazaar, almost as skinny and filthy as he'd been when they first took him in, or else meditating in various places around the city, like the star of a *Where's Waldo?* for spiritual expats. This must have been the phase when he wrote me the note about the Batras. A spiritual nomad, wandering the streets with his pajamas and Thermos, just sane enough to duck into an Internet café and terrify me.

And did he ever, I asked Cecilia, mention anything about a girl named Mira or a family named the Batras? (Saying her name out loud, which I'd never done with anyone other than Thomas, felt bizarre and reckless, like walking naked up to the hostess at a restaurant.)

"No, I don't think so. Who are they?"

"I'm not sure. He just mentioned them in a couple of emails."

"Sorry. He almost never talked about his personal life. It's hard to think of him even having one."

What seems weirdest to me, in retrospect (one of the many things that seems weird to me), is how readily I accepted all this, how little I wondered at it being *my* Thomas Pell these people were talking about. I seemed to be carrying into waking life something like the attitude I took when I was dreaming.

Which in some sense I guess I was: I'd seen a bejeweled, wet-eyed elephant (guest of honor at a wedding party) lumbering along the side of a highway. I'd seen a three-story statue of a He-Man monkey towering over a town square in which shrink-wrapped Paulo Coelho books were arranged on card tables next to copies of *Mein Kampf*. I'd seen a bearded, half-naked man crawling on all fours, except his hands were twisted inward, so really he was dragging himself along with his elbows; a little girl with scarred lumps where her eyes should have been; a woman whose head seemed to have been held in a fire. At some point the sleeping/waking distinction had begun to blur.

But still: people from Dupont Prep, people who'd never missed a meal in their lives unless they had to make up a test during lunch—people like that didn't end up homeless and half dead in Delhi. It just didn't happen.

Except apparently to Thomas.

He'd told me once, when we were fourteen, that the only belief system he'd ever been able to take seriously was empiricism (I'd nodded thoughtfully, and made a note to check Encarta when I got home). Well, the data were clear: the only people who had any idea what had happened to him were the types who keep Ziploc baggies of bee pollen on the kitchen counter and have their minds unselfconsciously blown by *Zen and the Art of Motorcycle Maintenance*. Apparently I needed to take whatever I thought I knew about him, whatever I thought I knew about what he would or wouldn't do, and toss it into the blue-smoking garbage fire I passed each afternoon on my way back to the apartment.

From: <Thomas Pell>
To: <Adam Sanecki>
Date: Sat, Jun 20, 2009 at 2:56 AM
Subject: re: (no subject)

. . . Until I was twenty-one I had never, I don't think you
could say, experienced true fear, of course I knew conventional fear, I'd known fear of being caught, but never
as a bodily emergency, never so overwhelming that you'd
kill yourself just to end it if you could only move. The first
was on a date, a girl I wanted very much to impress, I'd
worn a blazer, I became afraid, we were at a movie in
Lincoln Center, I became convinced sitting in the dark
that I had left the iron plugged in back in my room. More
and more certain, until I couldn't see the screen, I smelled
smoke, I saw the boy who lived next to me on fire, I could
see his cheeks burning, his lips melting, his teeth bare as
a skull, I ran from the theater, north on Broadway, couldn't
speak, fought through crowds, thinking of jail, thinking of
grief, telling his parents, my life would end, and there was
nothing, of course, it wasn't plugged in at all, but I didn't

feel relief, I felt empty . . . After that I could see each fear coming, small in the distance, fear of cancer, fear of being mugged, fear of loneliness, fear of insanity, then closer and closer, larger and larger, I dreaded them, begged myself please no, I wouldn't be able to move, would have to lie in bed and shake, I never knew cold sweats, each morning I would wake up with wet sheets, meanwhile classes, meanwhile tests, meanwhile I couldn't sleep, night was the worst, I'd never been afraid of the dark, you know, suddenly I'd sleep with the door open, or in the library, once or twice out on one of the lawns, a security guard told me to move along, thought I was homeless, I showed him my ID, he didn't care, thought I was drunk. Fear is muscular, cardiovascular, I had never been so tired, constant ache of having just been sick, constant dread, fear of fear. I would think, in quiet moments, how did I once meet people, walk down sidewalks, stand in elevators, how did I go about unterrified, what a miracle, what a feat, all these people uncelebrated in every room, they could do what I couldn't, no one appreciates the stacking of days, the launching of a personal space shuttle, we who can't, we *Challenger* explosions, shake in bed, stare at our knuckles. They don't tell you, no one does, that losing your mind is, more than anything else, terrifying . . .

From: <Sally Pell>
To: <Adam Sanecki>
Date: Mon, Jul 13, 2009 at 8:12 AM
Subject: re: thank you

I'm afraid in any honest version of these past few years
we're going to come across as just about the most naive
people on Earth. For our sakes, just keep in mind how
much we wanted to believe he was all right.

For much too long (easy to say now), we figured this was
a blip. Our Thomas would never drop out of school! This
was the boy who used to make us all read short stories
together instead of watching TV. This was the pride of AP
Chemistry.

So getting him off to college, we really thought we'd
done it, we'd gotten this package out into the world. After
we moved him into his dorm we stopped for dinner in
New Jersey, and I just looked at Richard and said, "Now
what?" Because for eighteen years we'd been following
this recipe. Giving him trumpet lessons; hiring tutors; tak-

ing him to plays; reading him books; driving his carpool; tying his shoes; zipping his jacket; wiping his bottom; drying his tears; cooling his fevers; removing his warts; trimming his hair. And now we were done! He was grown up.

But then he came home, and I just couldn't believe that this twenty-one-year-old needed more help than he had when he was eleven. You know something strange I'd sometimes think? That he might be faking. Or not faking, but playing up the drama of things a little, as part of the genius act. He was always so self-aware about that type of thing, how old Einstein had been when he'd gone off to college, all that.

. . . You do feel awfully embarrassed, bad as that sounds. At first I'd lie to people. I'd hear neighbors say they'd seen him going to the mailbox (that was as far as he'd go, at first) and I'd say he was just home for a visit. Some people didn't recognize him. Anne Wicker (she lives on Macomb, knew Thomas since he was five years old) asked did we have a relative in town, because she'd seen a skinny guy with a beard. Sometimes I was so mad I couldn't look at him. I wanted to say, Don't you know there are people in the world with actual diseases? Don't you know how much hurt you're causing your father? Sometimes I didn't recognize him. It just wasn't our Thomas.

He'd been home for maybe six months when we first heard him going out at night. I remember thinking, Good Lord, what next? So I sent Richard out to follow him. I figured what he was doing was going out and buying drugs. He'd sworn up and down he wasn't on any, but I just couldn't think what else made sense. I had the whole TV movie in my head: flushing things down toilets, tying him to the bed, really having it out.

But all he was doing, it turned out, was walking. Just like you two used to do, except alone. He'd walk a few blocks, stop in front of somebody's house, lie down, get up again. One of those mornings I said, "We heard you going out last night."

"Oh."

I said, "Where'd you go?"

"For a walk."

I cried like I hadn't in years, once we really knew it wasn't drugs. Can you imagine?

A problem with trying to accomplish anything when you're visiting a place like Delhi is that just living, getting up in the morning and staying on your feet until it's time to go to bed at night, feels like such an accomplishment already. I felt like the world's most incompetent private detective. Only instead of my incompetence turning out to be a tricky sort of asset, where I'd stumble onto the bad guys in their lair like the Pink Panther, I was going to end up stabbed and tubercular in a gutter, picked over by wild dogs, no closer to finding Thomas than if I'd never left D.C.

Never mind finding Thomas; just finding the hotel where I was supposed to meet Guruji's assistant (this was the major chore of my first week) somehow turned into a three-hour adventure. First the auto-rickshaw driver (auto-rickshaws were what people called the Flintstones cars, it turned out) misheard the address I gave him and took me, through unspeakable traffic, to Chandni Chowk when I wanted to be taken to Barahkhamba Road. Then, once I'd found another auto-rickshaw to take me back, and once I'd finally found the right street, the hotel turned out to be three-quarters closed due to construction. Then, trying to find somewhere to email Raymond to say I'd be late, I got lost in the electronics/ Styrofoam district, and by the time I made it back to the hotel, another entrance had been marked off with caution tape. I was never unsweaty. I was never rested. I was never entirely uninterested in finding a bathroom.

In a roundabout way, all this difficulty was reassuring. If I, sane and healthy and armed with *Lonely Planet: India,* was finding Delhi hard to navigate, then Thomas must have found it impossible. He could no more have found the Batras, assuming they were really there, than he could have found a particular pebble on the beach.

But of course I couldn't mention reassurance to the Pells. My dispatches, which I usually sent from an Internet café on the second floor of a coffee shop around the corner from the *barsati,* must have read like the journal entries Scott wrote as he was dying in the South Pole.

> Another day of sweating and frustratingly little news
> about Thomas. I seem to be getting sick, so may try to
> get an appointment with a doctor. Electricity broken in the
> apartment.

> Walked around Old Delhi today, where Thomas appar-
> ently did one of his "retreats." One of the most insane and
> overwhelming places I've ever been. Very steamy tonight.
> Electricity still spotty. No word on if/when I'll be able to
> see Sri P.

I never knew how much to say to them; they'd known bits about Thomas and his guru beforehand, from their own calls to people who'd lived in the apartment, but they hadn't known the details of his being homeless, or anything about the retreats. Out of Lost Boys solidarity, or maybe just out of cowardice, no one in the apartment had wanted to tell his parents much about what he'd been doing, and it turned out that I didn't either.

But for myself, for the purposes of my own search, I'd been spending most of my time trying to meet Guruji. If I was going to say that I'd made a real effort to find Thomas—if I was going to go back to D.C. feeling any less ashamed of myself than when I'd left—then I needed to at least talk to him. But apparently meeting Guruji wasn't going to be any easier than anything else; he'd been sick now for a month. Something with his heart, apparently, that people kept explaining by using a word that sounded like *bicuspid*. (At the *barsati* they'd been burning joss sticks and taking turns reading his old talks out loud.)

But Guruji was definitely still in Delhi, Cecilia said; he'd never left the city in his life, and he'd never been to a hospital. He also didn't use a phone or computer, so if you wanted to reach him, you had to write to Raymond, the man who handled all his worldly affairs.

From: <Adam Sanecki>
To: <RBrough132@aol.com>

Hi Raymond—

I'm a friend of Thomas Pell's, and I was wondering if it might be possible for me to meet with Sri Prabhakara sometime in the next few days.

Thanks in advance for your help,

Adam Sanecki

From: <RBrough132@aol.com>
To: <Adam Sanecki>

Vnerabl SP's time v limtd, apol, mtng not poss. [stat: UNCONFIRMED.]

From: <Adam Sanecki>
To: <RBrough132@aol.com>

Hi Raymond—

I'm not sure I understood your email. I realize Sri Prabhakara must have lots of people tugging at his sleeve,
but I'd hugely appreciate it if you would give some more
thought to whether it would be possible for me to meet
with him, even just for a few minutes. I'm not hoping for
a spiritual consultation; I'm interested in talking with him
about Thomas Pell, who I have good reason to think may
be in some sort of trouble.

Thanks,

Adam Sanecki

From: <RBrough132@aol.com>
To: <Adam Sanecki>

Pls snd q's IN WRITING- *VSP* v busy, face-to-f mtng not
poss- stndrd proc re all official inq's- [stat, pending frther
rev: UNCONFIRMED]

From: <Adam Sanecki>
To: <RBrough132@aol.com>

Hi Raymond—

I don't have a list of questions (I'm not any sort of official),
so I think this would be a lot easier in person. I'm not
a reporter or detective or anything else—my interest is
purely personal.

Thanks again for your help,

Adam Sanecki

From: <RBrough132@aol.com>
To: <Adam Sanecki>

VSP hlth v poor- intvw (WRITTEN/SPKEN) at pres imposs-
[stat: UNCONFIRMED]

This went on for days, like a meander through the circles of customer service hell, until finally, just an hour after he'd written to me for a third time to say that no meeting would be possible, Raymond sent an email with the subject line "URGENT":

From: <RBrough132@aol.com>
To: <Adam Sanecki>

VSP requests mtng- mo 3/8 14:30 - Cont Hotel sw side-
V IMP: NO CAMERA- NO REC EQUIP- CLEAN SHOES-
OFFRING OF VALRH 85% DRK CHOC- [20oz]- car to
wait [stat: CONF. PENDING]

So, just before two p.m. on my seventh day in India, after hours of auto-rickshaws and traffic cones, I stood alone outside what I was fairly sure was the southwest entrance of the Continental Hotel, wearing Rory's basically clean size-nine penny loafers. In a plastic bag I had a worrisomely softening Valrhona chocolate bar, the procuring of which had been a morning's work. I kept mistaking the tickle of sweat on my nose for a bug. Just when I was getting ready to go back into the lobby to see if I could convince the woman at the front desk to let me use the business center, an auto-rickshaw pulled to a stop and a disheveled, white-haired stork of a man unfolded himself from the passenger's seat.

"Adam? Raymond Broughton. In we go; you sit in back, please. Just shove my stick off the side. Drive, drive, drive."

Raymond was British; he looked to be about eighty, and he seemed to have dressed for a safari weeks or months ago and then not bothered to change. Stray feathers of white hair flapped from the sides of his head; his glasses made his eyes look like things preserved in jars. We were going straight to Guruji's home, apparently. Raymond couldn't have given me the address over email, of course. There were people who would very much like to know where Sri Prabhakara laid his head, as I must have known. The government was terribly frightened of him, terribly frightened, ever since the campaign in '84. Whether I ended up speaking to Guruji would of course depend on how he happened to be feeling just then, and there was quite a good chance, unfortunately, that he might not be feeling well at all. Sometimes these notions did overtake him; his ambitions were greater than his health. Was I staying at the Continental? That was the only place Raymond ever allowed guests to stay, because at all the rest of the hotels in central Delhi you were assured of being robbed, either by bandits or by the room rates. Was I familiar with Guruji's forty-four precepts and twelve injunctions?

While he talked he rummaged through my plastic bag and pulled out the chocolate bar, which he unwrapped and began to eat. "Dreadful for my teeth, really, but vital for the rest of me." Whenever our auto-rickshaw stopped or even slowed down, he slapped the back of the driver's seat and barked, "*Chalo! Chalo! Chalo!*" pointing in the direction of an alleged gap in the traffic. "They benefit from a bit of force, you know. Wonderful people but absolutely complacent."

We drove along a wide, dusty road through a part of town that looked something like Embassy Row in D.C., past trees with seedpods like brown leather baseballs. Guruji's building turned out to be half an hour from the hotel, in a neighborhood that looked like an American suburb, if that suburb had been fending off an invasion. All the lawns were *Wizard of Oz* green and newly mowed, and at the base of every driveway, in front of a wall topped with chicken wire or broken glass, stood a bored-looking security guard in a blue uniform.

At the end of a cul-de-sac, in front of a beige three-story building, Raymond leaped out and rushed past the guard without so much as a nod. Outside the door he directed me to speak very quietly ("Guruji may well have reconsidered, you understand") and then led me up into an apartment no bigger, but much cleaner, than the *barsati*. All the curtains were drawn, so it was dark inside; the floorboards were buckled and loose, the doorframes seemed to tilt. There was a low dresser covered in incense holders (hence the sweet, slightly sickening smell in the air) and, above it, a wall covered in mismatched framed photos of men who looked very much as if they might have been called Sri. There was a beatific dark-skinned man with wavy Jesus hair gazing upward; a wizened homunculus of a man seated cross-legged in an orange robe; a white-bearded man laughing and tilting his head.

Raymond was the kind of person whose whisper is just as loud, and maybe more piercing, than his ordinary speaking voice. "I'm just going to step in and see how he's doing, if you'll excuse me."

As a little kid I'd gone with my mom on a few visits to a dying great-aunt in Connecticut, and the feeling in Guruji's apartment—the hush and stillness—brought those awkward afternoons back. That and maybe the closed bedroom door, behind which I could hear murmuring voices now, not just Raymond's, and some sort of low staticky chatter.

After long enough that I wondered if I'd been forgotten, and whether I'd remember how to get back to the main road to catch an auto-rickshaw, Raymond cracked open the door and hissed, "Come now, please. Shoes off."

I'm not exactly sure how I would have pictured a spiritual guru's bedroom (maybe a buckwheat mat, a hanging gong), but it wasn't like this. An enormous bed with four dark carved posts as tall as the ceiling; overlapping Oriental rugs; gauzy curtains; a dozen burning candles scattered over brass tables and dark wooden dressers. A founding father could have died in this room. The air was like miso soup; the chatter turned out to be coming from a black-and-white TV with a broken antenna, tuned to a soap opera set in a hospital.

Sitting in a tall, carved chair right next to the bed was a man who must have been the doctor; he had John Lennon glasses and a dark mustache and an actual white doctor's jacket. He looked down at his feet like someone who wished he could be elsewhere or, barring that, invisible. Standing behind him, slowly flapping a woven fan in the direction of the bed, was a woman I took to be a nurse; she wore something multilayered and a white face mask, and seemed determined not to look at me.

And there in the bed, tucked carefully under the covers like an E.T. doll, lay Sri Prabhakara. He was as dark skinned a person as I'd seen in India, and at least as old as Raymond. He had a silver shine where he'd once had hair, and a calm, vaguely amused expression. His head was much too big for his body, and his ears and nose were much too big for his face. What I could see of his chest was covered in white cotton; next to him on the bed sat a rusting silver bell. He'd been looking at the TV, but now he turned his eyes to me in a way that made me think of a long-suffering sea turtle.

"Alone, please," he said. Or mouthed; his voice was just at the edge of what I could hear. "TV, off." The nurse and doctor began to go and Raymond held the door for them.

"Shall I go too," Raymond said, "or would you like me to stay, in case . . ."

"Go."

"Of course."

As soon as the door was closed, leaving just the two of us, I was filled with the same fluttery, empty-headed feeling I've had the few times I've been around celebrities. Waiting for popcorn behind Cal Ripken in a Cleveland Park movie theater, standing next to Diane Keaton at baggage claim in the Denver airport; it was that kind of feeling. Guruji gestured with a shaky hand for me to sit in the doctor's chair. From up close I could smell a peppery balm and something like sage.

"You are . . . nervous. Why?"

"Well, I don't think I'm really nervous, just sort of, you know, sorry, it's a little weird, I only came, I don't know if Raymond told you, my friend Thomas? I think you might have known him—"

"Breathing . . . please."

"Sorry. I'm just . . . Do you think I could maybe ask you a little bit about Thomas, because his parents actually—"

"First . . . the calm body. Beginning . . . to consider . . . hearing . . . sounds . . . the moving air . . . the birds outside . . ." (I didn't hear any birds, but for the first time since coming to India, I could hear the ticking of my watch.) "One hundred . . . breaths. Feeling . . . feeling." He let his eyes fall shut, and I worried he might have died. But then he said, "One? . . . One. Two? . . . Two." With every breath a single crimped nose hair shook.

"Thirty-one? . . . Thirty-one. Thirty-two? . . . Thirty-two." He counted as slowly and steadily as a roof leak. By the time we got to a hundred I'd passed through disbelief and outrage and arrived at something like acceptance, as if I were listening to one of my tutees mangling an interminable joke. *I'm sitting at the bedside of an Indian guru who's counting to a hundred with his eyes closed. This is in fact what's happening.*

"Now . . . calm?"

"Yes, much better, thank you."

"You see? Is . . . available . . . always."

"That's very useful, thank you."

"Now . . . question?"

I told him that I'd come here, all the way from America, because I was looking for my friend Thomas Pell. Did he know Thomas?

"Yes, I know Thomas-ji . . . very much."

Good. Various people had told me that he was the person

to talk to, and if he could shed any light on where Thomas might have gone, when he'd disappeared a few weeks ago, I'd be deeply grateful, and so would his parents, who are of course . . .

"Who tell you . . . has disappeared?" (Now I noticed that Guruji was missing most of his top teeth.)

Well, an old student of his named Cecilia had told me, most recently. And I'd actually been in touch with Thomas earlier in the summer, until he'd all of a sudden stopped writing. But if Thomas hadn't disappeared, then by all means, he should please tell me where he was.

"You . . . do not . . . watch . . . the self. Suffer . . . very much. Thomas-ji say to me."

"Thomas told you something about me?"

"Precept . . . seventeen. Before the mind . . . can be . . . clear . . . the guilt must be . . ." He made a gesture like someone pulling out a vegetable by the roots. "You act, but do not . . . understand."

"If you could maybe just tell me whatever you—" I was having trouble, all of a sudden, distinguishing between the sound of my watch and the feeling of my heartbeat. I was like the crocodile in *Peter Pan* who swallows a clock.

"Thomas-ji . . . did . . . very bad. Very harmful . . . thing. Young woman . . . years ago. You know this, yes?"

"I . . . yes, I know this." For some reason lying wasn't a possibility.

"Before . . . can escape . . . must confess. Before . . . can confess . . . must purify . . . intention. *Noida*. You understand?"

"No." I felt, suddenly, as if I were in danger of bursting into tears, and I was fairly sure that Guruji recognized it, and maybe even that he'd intended it.

"Day . . . please?"

"Today? Today's Monday. The, um, third. August third."

"Moon . . . please?"

"The moon? I don't know. I don't know what you mean."

He shut his eyes again, and I only noticed after a few seconds that he was counting something on his fingertips against the bedspread. "Tuesday . . . four. Wednesday . . . five. Thursday . . . six. Friday . . . seven. Vesak moon coming Monday . . . ten. Right condition . . . for cave *puja* . . . The beginning August is . . . for you, for Thomas . . . very important, yes?"

If I'd been at full strength in that moment, there were a hundred things I would have asked, but I had to use all my energy not to faint. I could have been breathing through the straw in a juice box.

Now Sri Prabhakara let his head fall to the side, so he was facing me directly, and he reached out to touch the back of my hand, which was trembling on my knee.

"You know . . . I, Sri Prabhakara . . . I am . . . close. Three month . . . four month. Short time."

"You're sick, yes, I've heard. I'm sorry."

He waved his hand. "Doctor try to give me . . . medicines. I do not. Pain . . . is OK. Dying . . . is OK. Your friend Thomas-ji. You must help him . . . purify. You understand?"

"No."

"Is . . . pure. Nothing . . ." He made a gesture like wiping something off his hands.

"I just want to know where he is."

"Bring me . . . candle. Two candle . . . there."

His tone of requesting something was the same as his tone of explaining something, so it took me a second to realize what he wanted, but I stood up and grabbed the two white candles from the table behind me; they were the size of saltshakers. He took them lightly in his crabbed hands and blew out the one on the right.

"You see?"

"I don't think so."

Now he relit the extinguished candle with the still-burning one in his left hand. There was a knocking at the door, and Raymond's voice saying something, but neither of us looked up.

"Now . . . you see?"

"I'm sorry, no."

"Is new candle . . . is same fire. Your friend . . . Thomas-ji . . . when you help . . . purify . . . when I am away . . . he is the new. You see?"

From: <Thomas Pell>

To: <Adam Sanecki>

Date: Thu, Jun 25, 2009 at 5:01 AM

Subject: re: (no subject)

. . . Here's something I don't think you know, I kept her obituary in the locked drawer of my desk, I would look at it, alone at night, she smiled like someone had made an old joke, she wore glasses, someone outside the frame had his arm around her, I would imagine I knew her, it was my arm, sometimes I could hear her voice, I could feel her sweater against my cheek, I'd shake like a tuning fork. To my parents I must have looked like I was doing nothing, lying on the couch, turning to face away from the sun, I could have been paralyzed, I could have been a house-plant, inside I was screaming, the fear was worse, when your mind turns against you, the felt experience, I didn't know, was that the world turns against you. I wanted to see her parents, wanted to ask were they all right, had they lived their lives, I wondered if I'd taken their suffer-ing (matter is neither created nor destroyed). I knew I was

evil, I'd been a mistake, if I lived as I was, continued to
live, I was a spinning blade, a driverless car. Not sleeping for days, I would have conversations with Mira, see
her sitting with me on the couch, whispering to me, the
back of her head was missing, she didn't know, I would
sit up sobbing, tell R I didn't know why, must have been
a nightmare, he would hold my head in his lap, I'd never
known my parents, something had gone cold, these
people I'd loved were strangers, obstacles, I needed to
stop feeling the way I felt, endless planning. I would try,
sometimes, to test whether parts were still OK, I would
take down a book from the shelf, the sentences would
close up as I read them, I would forget the meaning by
each period. I would turn on the TV, daytime movies, I
couldn't follow plots, what plots I could understand had
to do with terror, death, exposure. Sometimes I needed a
blanket, I became cold, much colder than the temperature. Other days the floor, the couch was too soft, I would
need my face against wood, I would quietly moan, feel the
buzz, I would ask the floor, Did I deserve to live, if I did,
please tell me how, please tell me how Adam manages.
This lasted months. I started to walk sometimes at night
to their house, 3409 Ordway, leaving my front door like
walking into a fire, such terror, I would stare at my feet,
every step, fifteen minutes, a street just like yours, red
brick, shingle roof, the lights were off, island in the ocean,
I thought of her parents asleep in their beds, I thought of
her childhood room untouched, I would lie on the lawn
by their brick path, imagine she was buried underneath,
flesh turned sod, I would think, How will I get home, will
I be found here, will I be buried here. I saw myself, clear
as a photograph, locked away somewhere, white walls,
blue skin, life as a disease that must run its course, and
I decided if I wasn't going to end up there, I needed
to be punished, killed or forgiven, otherwise the world
would do it, otherwise nights of fear, worse than death.

I started to sleep, sometimes, outside their house, praying
for courage, imagining pressing the bell, moving closer
each night to their front door. Grass is wet even when it
doesn't rain, I'd forgotten, one night, walking close to the
window, I tripped, made a sound, I saw lights come on,
my legs were burning, my moment had come, I heard
doors unlocking, it was four in the morning. The man in
the door was white, he wore a green robe, white beard,
he said what the hell was I doing, I just stared, mind blank
as paper, he said get away or he'd call the police, I said,
Is this the Batras' house? He stared, squinting, What? I
said, The Batras, do the Batras live here? Who? he said,
I said the name again, his face changed, the porch light
was golden, there was a basket of soccer balls, he said,
They moved, they moved away, now get out of here, and
slammed the door, I walked home, wet socks, cold hands,
I tried to run, couldn't think, could hardly stand, cats
crossed my path, it didn't matter, my luck couldn't get
worse, I needed to find out where the Batras had gone, I
couldn't rest until I knew.

From: \<Richard Pell\>
To: \<Adam Sanecki\>
Date: Wed, Jul 15, 2009 at 9:19 PM
Subject: re: greetings

Those first couple of years when he was back home,
we lived at doctors' offices. My dreams were full of waiting rooms, insurance forms, jars of tongue depressors.
Nothing quite as disillusioning as those appointments—
you could die of hope, just the way one of those clever
quotable people said about Hollywood. His GP—
overmatched pink-faced man—did a thousand dollars
of tests and told us Thomas should drink Ensure to
regain some weight. A Bethesda shrink—office full of
tribal masks and tissue boxes—spent six months finding out that Thomas didn't talk until he was two. One
great coup of Sally's was an appointment with an NIH
neurologist—pompous whisperer in a lab coat, Nobel
craver—who ran tests, found nothing, then recom-
mended that we see the shrink he'd stopped seeing
months before.

Daily mechanics felt like we'd slipped fifteen years
backward—elementary school sick days, stacks of books,
untouched toast on a plate. The living-room couch was
his alpha and omega. He'd lie there, beatific, Christ
thin, not moving. Getting him anywhere—the doctor, the
shower, the kitchen table—was like reeling in a marlin.
I'd forgotten, since my mother—she had MS, before
anyone knew what it was—the time signature of sickness,
how each day is endless but you look up and a year's
passed, suddenly your son has been on the couch for two
winters.

He and I would do these Pinter plays—me on the edge of
the couch, him staring at the ceiling fan.

"What's up? What're you feeling?"

"I don't know."

"All right, so what's that like?"

"It's unpleasant. I would like to be left alone, please."

"We can do that, but look, here's the deal. You're in our
house, you're getting fed, you've got a roof . . ." My
father's words, my lips. Then I'd go weep in the bathroom
until it was time to start on dinner.

At some point every leaf-blowing neighbor, concerned
cousin, FedEx man had given us their "take"—overlapping
soliloquies of advice. I became a good nodder.

"It's because of the expectations he's had on him, this is
just his way of saying, Whoa, let's make sure I'm doing
what I'm doing for myself and not my parents."

"So often when this kind of thing happens you dig and
dig, thinking there's something psychological or medi-
cal at the bottom of it, and actually it turns out to just be
some cute brunette . . ."

"You must know, but this is the age . . . Men between nineteen and twenty-five. My nephew's roommate in Boston . . ."

Sally and I strapped on horse blinders: small victories, days not worse than the day before—OK, he drank half a smoothie. He asked me to hand him the computer. I haven't heard him going out for walks at night. And then, just when we'd started to think, you know, this may be it, the life of our son, Thomas announced he'd applied for a job—I had to actually hold myself up on the back of the chair. He wanted money of his own, he said. Independence. He'd been printing out applications, making calls. And so now Thomas—reader of Kant, Most Likely to . . .— got a job behind the counter at the Subway on MacArthur, $6.75 an hour. And we were weak with joy.

Again, a slip back in time—this time to first days of school, nervous bus-watching. He refused to be driven to work, so he walked forty minutes each morning, already in his green uniform—he'd had to get one for women, the men's small hung on him like a tarp. I went a couple of times for lunch, half spy, half customer, he'd be there turning on the ovens, pouring the chopped pickles, stacking the coffee lids. No hello. I'd watch him make a sandwich, slow as folding a flag. Watch him watching "chicken" rotate in the microwave, his head cocked. And after six weeks he got fired. Or maybe quit—not clear, wouldn't explain. Something to do with a customer he didn't like, or with refusing to change his gloves. This was the first of the jobs—Blockbuster, Papa John's, Kate's Paperie—which got to have a feeling of . . . slipping even further back, watching him cross a room, eighteen months old, knowing he's going to fall, knowing I've got to let him . . . He needed money, he kept saying. Something of his own.

Until that visit to Sri Prabhakara, I'd treated the possibility that Thomas might have found the Batras mainly as a thing in need of ruling out. In D.C., in the day or two before I decided to go, I'd done a couple of deliberately hopeless Google searches, to prove to myself that finding them would be impossible. And then once I saw Delhi, once I'd waded into the crowds and chaos, I'd lowered the chances even more; my job here was just going to be finding Thomas and bringing him home, or (more likely) declaring him unfindable and heading home myself with a sad story and a clear conscience (or at least a no-less-clear-than-before conscience). By the time I'd been there for a few days, I thought that he had a better chance of being dead than he did of having found what he was looking for.

But Guruji's whispering had struck a match in me; I spent Tuesday pacing around the neighborhood feeling not much less fevered than Thomas, more and more convinced with every sweaty hour that he really was going to confess to the Batras, if he hadn't done it already. Is there a name for a version of hypochondria in which, instead of being convinced you have a disease, you're convinced that the thing you'd least like to happen is unfolding just outside your view? Every thought I had seemed to tug on the ends of a knot in my intestines. I'd known, of course, at some depths of my brain, that my trip would cover the anniversary of the accident, but the date had always been like a dead key on a piano; I did my best to play around it, or to speed on as if it didn't exist. But now the dead key, the hollow tapping, was all I could hear. *I'm getting ready, when it's time I will do what needs to be done . . .*

I spent hours in the coffee shop/Internet café, doing exactly the kind of research I'd spent the past twelve years avoiding. The computer had a greasy mouse pad with a drawing of a butterfly riding a lion. My mouth tasted strongly of bitter, cold coffee, which I kept trying to fix by taking more sips of bitter, cold coffee. *Manish Batra Amita Batra New Delhi. Manish Batra Amita Batra Washington D.C. New Delhi car crash.* I sent emails to Raymond (*Do you think I could possibly meet with Guruji again? Would he be willing to talk on the phone?*) that I immediately wished I could take back. I even checked my old girlfriend Claire's Facebook page, just to leave no seed of unhappiness unwatered. (*Check out new half marathon pics— gotta love the short shorts!*) Driving yourself insane on the Internet is as easy as checking the weather.

Almost everything I managed to pull up about the Batras was nonsense: law associate listings, LinkedIn profiles, academic papers, consumer fraud websites. Maybe finding them really was hopeless. Maybe Thomas was right then babbling a confession to the Hanuman statue in Karol Bagh. But at some point on Wednesday night, when I was sitting at a computer in the back corner of the café, carving out new lows for myself on an hourly basis, I found what I was looking for, or what I was looking away from. It was in the June/July 2001 newsletter of the Hindu Temple of Greater D.C. This was where they'd held Mira's memorial service (one of my first searches had turned up the ancient *Washington Post* story with the death announcement). My stomach wobbled as I sat waiting for the PDF to load, breathing through flared nostrils. *WARNING:*

3 Minutes Remaining in Session, Click HERE to Purchase 15 Extra Minutes.

On the front of the newsletter, above a message from HTGDC president Deepika Sharma, was a logo like a Mardi Gras elephant sitting on a throne. The community announcements were printed in columns on the second-to-last page.

> As many of you know the strong and committed support of Manish and Amita Batra has been integral to our temple growing in leaps and bounds in these past fifteen years. It is therefore with heavy hearts that we must ask you to join us and say "farewell" and also "good wishes" as they prepare to leave the HTGDC community and return to New Delhi, where family and great opportunities await. May the remover of all obstacles bless Manish and Amita as he blesses you all.
>
> Many have asked questions as regarding the progress of the Rathi Spiritual Center, which we can happily tell you continues to advance rapidly with thanks to the generous work of . . .

There should be studies done on the relationship between panic and bowel urgency. Within seconds of reading the newsletter, I was, for the fifth time that day, locked in the paper-towel-less unisex bathroom, trembling and sweating as if, on top of everything else, I had giardia. Being a human, having a body, can be such a terrible thing.

I ran back to the apartment, past the hubcap heap and the man selling bananas for one rupee each, clutching the newsletter printout with wet hands, looking for Rory so I could borrow his phone. I kept having to remind myself that all I'd learned was that the Batras had moved back; Thomas still wouldn't have been able to find them; they might even have moved again. But my inner organs weren't having any of it.

Rory was eating a bowl of Ready Brek at the kitchen table. "No worries, no worries," he said, standing up, wiping his mouth. His crappy little blue phone worked only if you took it up to the roof and stood hunched in the corner that overlooked an alley full of old planks. The night was thick and breezy; under the layers of car exhaust it felt almost tropical.

I pressed the dozen or so numbers, waited through a series of beeps, and then adjusted the angle of my hunching until the ringing came into focus. It was nine and a half hours earlier in D.C. than in Delhi, which is to say that for the woman who finally answered the phone at the Hindu Temple of Greater D.C. it was just after ten in the morning.

"Yes, hello, good morning, Hindu Temple?"

"Hi, I'm calling with a question about a cousin of mine who used to belong to your temple?"

"Yes, hello, good morning, Hindu Temple?"

"Hi, I'm calling with a question about one of your former members?"

"Oh, hello, yes. Membership question?"

For the next fifteen minutes (minutes that cost me more than every bite of food I'd eaten so far in India), I lied that I was named Sanjay Batra, repeated again and again the story of how I'd left my address book in a cab, waited on hold while the woman talked to her coworkers, and kept my brain, or anyway my eyes, busy by staring at the acne-pitted moon rising behind an electricity tower.

"Oh yes," the woman said, after an especially long hold, "Manish Batra and Amita Batra, they move back to India, two thousand two. Move away. No more in Washington."

"Yes, and do you have an address for them?"

"Address for them, sorry?"

More holding, more swelling string music, more moon-staring.

"OK, yes, sir, I have forwarding address, Manish Batra, Amita Batra. You have a pencil ready?"

I had a British Airways pen and the back of a newsletter

and a trembling knee. I looked like someone taking down the number of a pizza place and I felt like someone learning the date of his death. *Manish and Amita Batra, D-5, Sector 8, Noida, India.*

So *Noida* wasn't a Sanskrit word for purification. It was a place—a suburb an hour and a half outside of Delhi, it turned out—with its own map on page 839 of my guidebook. Good God.

The bus didn't leave until the next morning, so I had a full night to think about what I was doing. I didn't even lie down; instead I took a shower, which entailed switching on the electric heater and ignoring the smell of burning plastic, and then I sat, wearing my last clean clothes, in the kitchen under the fluorescent tube light, failing to read a Philip Dick novel I'd bought at a bookstall, drinking beer after beer in the hopes of settling my brain and killing whatever parasites were thriving in my stomach. I stood up every half hour to rediscover that there was nothing to eat in the fridge except hot sauce and a head of cauliflower. It's hard to reconstruct my mind's state now, but I don't think, if I'd really been forced to bet, that I would have said it was likely that I'd actually find Thomas or the Batras in Noida. I don't think I really thought I'd find anything. But it was like not being able to remember whether you locked your apartment door; it was like my entire trip: I needed, with a helplessness that felt like tumbling down a cliffside, to know for sure.

The bus depot in central Delhi, particularly on no sleep, particularly with a hangover, is as despair inducing a place as you're ever likely to encounter. Drivers stand in front of their buses, shouting the names of their routes and waving indecipherable timetables; Dantean beggars of every age and variety of misfortune root through garbage drifts; wooden-seated toilets overflow behind broken doors. It was eighty-nine degrees at nine thirty in the morning.

I somehow managed, after much gesticulating and stumbling and rushing from one side of the station to the other, to get on my bus. My seat was in the back, one of those shelf seats that folds down from the wall, and there was a better-than-even chance, I thought as we pulled out, that we were headed somewhere other than Noida, but by that point I couldn't have moved even if I'd wanted to. A dozen men with woven plastic suitcases stood crammed next to me in the aisle, and every few minutes we pulled over to pick up another group of men with woven plastic suitcases, until it felt like the bus's underside was scraping the road. I eventually fell asleep against my backpack in my lap, breathing through my mouth, the sun roasting the right half of my face a deep maroon. I could probably have made better time by walking.

I'd pictured Noida, based on the chirpy paragraph in my guidebook, as something like Tysons Corner: clean and fake and functional, golf courses and parking lots and new developments next to four-lane highways. But *clean* and *functional* turn out to be relative terms. We pulled into the station just past noon, and there were in fact office buildings, all swooping glass, that could have been built for insurance companies in Fairfax; but there were also traffic circles in which scarily muscled cows stood knee-deep in garbage and, off on a hillside, clusters of what looked like tepees made from plastic tarps. I'd been vaguely planning on either taking the last bus back to Delhi or else staying the night at the Noida Radisson, which was the only hotel listed in my guidebook, but what if I couldn't get a room? What if I missed my bus and ended up stuck and wandering these cloverleaf intersections? Maybe it wasn't wise to go to a city you'd never heard of without telling anyone your plans. Certain kinds of fear, along with certain states of hangover, make me hungry: within half an hour I was standing on a sidewalk in front of Domino's, eating a whole deluxe veggie pizza that it took me three slices to realize tasted like paprika.

Floating somewhere in the scummy lake of my thoughts was: Don't listen to your brain; you're just very tired. Thomas is probably passed out on the street in Delhi, or wandering through some other city entirely, scattering misleading emails behind him like birdseed. People who pass out on temple steps don't keep mental calendars.

I caught an auto-rickshaw in front of a Volkswagen dealership and handed the Batras' address to the driver. He studied it for a minute before he waggled his head, which I was finally beginning to understand didn't mean *no,* but instead meant something like, *If you insist, sir.*

Sector 8 turned out to be a ways away from the city center, in a part of town where there really were golf courses (empty ones surrounded on all sides by dirt pits) and gated condos with men gloomily sweeping the courtyards.

D-5 was on a street with short, shrubby trees and strips of dust and grass along the sidewalks. The sky was low and white; there were birds chattering in the trees; there was a man in a plaid shirt and rubber sandals walking along singing and bobbling a cell phone. The rupees I gave the driver were dark with sweat. I was now, to my bafflement, standing alone under a dusty tree, across the street from the house (which looked more like a motel or a compound) belonging to the family of the girl I'd killed twelve years ago. But exhaustion muddles everything. I was trembling, but I was also nauseated by the bitter film coating the inside of my mouth and distracted by a pressure at the back of my eye sockets that I worried might be the beginning of dengue fever.

I watched a trio of schoolkids in blue uniforms run past, throwing bits of gravel at each other. I watched a little brown bird wrestle with a chunk of bread. I watched an Audi with tinted windows pull out of the driveway a few houses down and speed off away from me. What I needed, really, if I wasn't going to fall asleep or throw up, was another beer. I'd brought the six-pack of Kalyani from next to the fridge, with the thought that I'd drink it that night in my hotel room, but desperate times, etc.

By three, which is to say by the time I'd stood there shakily under my tree for about forty-five minutes, one empty bottle now at my feet and another in my hand, I'd decided on something like a plan: I'd hang out near their house for the rest of the day, maybe at some point taking just enough of a nap to sharpen my thinking, and then, once I'd realized/resolved that the whole idea of Thomas being there was impossible, I'd take an auto-rickshaw back to town and catch the ten o'clock bus to Delhi. I'd never tell anyone, especially not the Pells, about this little trip to Noida, and I'd fly back to D.C. on Sunday. That would mean that I'd spent two weeks looking, which would have to count, for the Pells and for myself, as giving it the old college try. I'd leave Thomas to whatever purification or cave exploration he and Guruji deemed necessary, and I'd get back, as soon as possible, to the distant disaster that was my life.

I've never, of course, been a burglar, so I've never cased a house, but I think I now know, based on that afternoon/evening in Noida, more or less what it would be like. I couldn't sleep, as it turned out (every time I started to go under, I snapped awake, feeling like a bungee cord had saved me from a fall), so instead I set up a little stakeout fort and waited. My main base of operations was the space between a row of bushes and a low brick wall directly across the road from the Batras'. If you ever want to be transported back to being five years old, hide behind a bush for a few hours. I got to know the pattern of the leaves and the smell of the dirt and the feeling, against my knees and tailbone, of each rock in the vicinity. There were earthworms and red ants, neither of which showed the least bit of interest in the mini puddles of beer I poured for them. There were clouds moving over me like a slow-motion comb-over.

I don't think I ever stared so long at any of the buildings we studied in my Introduction to Architecture class in college; I don't think I ever stared so long at any house I ever lived in. I got to know the corrugated metal of D-5's leaky gutter; the brass or fake brass of its balconies; the dusty stones of its driveway; the spidery lines on the white wall where there had once been ivy. Could people really grieve behind those walls? Could they mourn while opening that broken mailbox? Being sleepless and half drunk was giving my thoughts a collage quality; I was as close as I'd ever come to the locked room in the basement of my life, and I was having to remind myself, over and over, the name of the city I was in.

Every hour or so I stood up and walked to the end of the street, trying to keep my legs from cramping up. I saw the full beginning, middle, and end of the man in D-11 washing his beige sports car. I saw guests arrive at D-6 with a casserole dish and leave with a ceramic bowl. I saw, and felt deep kinship with, a brown dog lying tied to a tree in front of D-1, staring and sleeping and waiting and sleeping and staring.

At one point behind the bush, my legs did fall asleep, all the way past tingling and pain and into the realm of immobility. By sunset, when the streetlights came on, I'd given up on walking, and I'd started feeling the individual grooves of parchedness on the roof of my mouth. I deeply regretted the beer I'd poured on the ground. In order not to waste any water (I had a quarter-full eight-ounce bottle of Nestlé Pure Life) I was parceling it out to myself, one warm capful per fifteen minutes. It was getting so dark in my stakeout fort that to check my watch I had to hold it so that it was almost brushing my eyelashes.

It was eight o'clock, at a moment when I happened to be busy unwrapping my third and final Nature Valley Oats 'n Honey bar, when a black Mercedes swung into D-5's driveway and three people stepped out: two paunchy men in short sleeves and a small gray-haired woman in a purple sari that went past her feet. The men were talking (I couldn't tell whether they were speaking English or Hindi) while the woman unlocked the door and led them inside. Could those be the Batras? Could that ten-second flash of faces and voices really be them? Suddenly I was sitting on my knees, a mound of unchewed granola in my mouth, staring as the light came on in the front hall. I held my breath. Why had I chosen a hiding place so directly across from their front windows? I felt like a squirrel frozen in conspicuousness on a tree trunk.

The light in another room came on, then went off. I thought I heard an inner door closing, maybe an air conditioner whirring to life.

It wasn't so much that I decided to miss the last bus back to Delhi as it was that I just watched the time come and go when I would have needed to stand up and leave for it. My watch said it was 8:45 and then that it was 9:20 and then that it was 10:15: time was tumbling down the cliffside next to me. I guess I'll just sleep here, I decided. Or not sleep here. Maybe I'm done with sleep; maybe my body's now learned how to make do on oats and anxiety. I should steal a letter to check their name, I thought. Wait for tomorrow's mail. I wonder if mailmen in India drive on the wrong side of the road—wait, do mailmen in America drive on the wrong side of the road, or is it just their steering wheels, steering, *steering* wheels . . . is *steering* really a word?

It was almost eleven when I first noticed that some minutes had passed that I couldn't account for. My head was doing that chemistry-class thing of drifting and snapping, drifting and snapping. So *now* I could sleep. I pinched myself on the thigh, which didn't keep me awake but did, along with my tipped-over water bottle, introduce into my dreaming a plotline about blood seeping through my pants, soaking the ground.

I'm not making excuses, really; I'm just trying to explain, or to understand, why it was that I didn't notice when it got to be midnight, and why it hadn't occurred to me that that was the time to wait for. It was now August 7. The auto-rickshaw only stopped in front of D-5's driveway for a few seconds. You'd think (I would certainly have thought) that I wouldn't have recognized Thomas at first. But even in the half-dark of the street, even with his body so thin and a beard covering most of his face, I knew him before his driver had pulled away. He couldn't have been fifty feet from me. He wore what looked like rumpled pajamas and no shoes. His hair was short but shaggy. I once heard a woman on the news who'd woken up to find her house on fire say that she hadn't known, even as she was running out to the street, whether she was dreaming, and I'd thought, That can't really be true. But I really didn't know as I sat there staring; as Thomas, in the light at the foot of the driveway, brought his palms together at his forehead and bowed, and then as he glided, smooth and solemn as a priest down an aisle, up the walkway and onto the porch. That must have been the moment I unfroze, because suddenly I was across the road and on the porch beside him, with my hand on his arm. The word on my tongue was something like *stop* or *wait* or *no*. But I didn't have a chance to open my mouth before he turned to me (his calm, his complete lack of surprise, was the most dreamlike part) and said, "You came." He was himself, minus twenty pounds and plus a beard in which you could have hidden a pencil. His eyes looked almost happy. His posture was weirdly rigid. I still hadn't spoken and it was already too late; his pointer finger hung in the air as if he were a skeleton delivering a warning. He'd rung the bell.

―――――

From: \<Thomas Pell\>
To: \<Adam Sanecki\>
Date: Sat, Jun 27, 2009 at 3:29 AM
Subject: re: (no subject)

You ask how, with such fear when I left the house, did I
leave the country, I started by degrees, trained myself,
habit is mechanical, a matter of currents, I decided ten
minutes outside in daylight today, walking to the corner, then an hour, our old creek path, then two hours,
then jobs, I needed money, this trip must be my own,
for bosses I could pretend to be ordinary, I would say,
Semester off, I would let S cut my hair, I would say,
Columbia, cross my legs, normalcy is a role, a series of
lines, then days of standing behind a counter, staring at
cash registers, counting minutes. Fear would rise and
I would tell myself, Bear it, welcome it, you can't run, I
would swim in fear like a wave, didn't hear bosses, cus-
tomers, tasted tears, heard a terrible roar. I needed two
thousand dollars, every moment was a footstep, whether
you want something or want to get away from something,

the wanting is the same, two years, the people I'd known
had jobs, were engaged, I knew until my ribs didn't show,
my parents would never let me travel, I ate peanut butter
and grapes, these too are habits, I didn't mention India,
didn't mention anything, began to say, I'm feeling better,
let's go to a movie, I'll see a doctor again, this one was
Dr. Lennard, marble lobby, elevator to six, I would sit in a
leather chair, air-conditioning and water pitcher, he had
framed pictures of antique cars, he would ask me how
had the conversation with my mother gone, when else
had I felt panic, what was my father's history of depression, I was Homer, remembered every story, I didn't lie,
presented evidence, Easter eggs in close-cut grass, the
pressure of school, the years of friendlessness, he nodded and nodded, touched his tie, had I considered, had
I ever thought about whether, yes. He shook my hand,
the ends of sessions, S and R in the waiting room, their
hopeful faces, He's very smart, I said, riding home, they
were so happy. S kissed my forehead, I felt wet lips, trust
was blooming, algae on a lake, my plans were swimming
underneath.

From: <Richard Pell>
To: <Adam Sanecki>
Date: Sat, Jul 18, 2009 at 8:44 PM
Subject: re: greetings

My worry never exactly dissipated—I'd still bolt upright in bed from dreams of slipknots—but hope began to flicker when it suddenly seemed—this was the development we'd been told to watch for, by professional horror-treaters—he *wanted to be well*. He was "engaging in his own treatment." Which refers not just to the jobs, but to finishing his plate at dinner. Taking showers. Referring to future things: "when I go back to school," "when I move out," even once (Sally cried, raced from the room) "when I have kids."

He'd started seeing Dr. Lennard, and we thought it had to be the medicine—blue pill for depression, period-sized white one for panic. I could have written sonnets to Pfizer and GlaxoSmithKline, odes to the roses in corporate New Jersey flower beds. For the first time since he'd been home Sally and I went out to dinner—asked for the check with our entrees, sudden gush of dread, but still, a step.

And then he'd mention travel—at first it was guidebooks on the coffee table, browser windows left open to Inca Trail tourist sites. We thought, Yes, please, to travel is to care, to refill your plate with experience. We thought, We must have misimagined his life, but no problem—we'll gladly be the parents stepping off a plane in a strange city, meeting a foreign wife, hearing grandchildren arguing in someone else's language. Compared with three months ago, when all we could think of was visiting a ward, a grave—we were in rapture.

So, India. Suddenly the focus was all India. And I began to—I've had time, an infinity of nighttime hours, to regret this—plug his enthusiasms into the amplifier of myself. India? Here's the best bio of the Buddha. Narayan novel. Account of independence. This churn is what I do. Will it be north or south? Work or study? When will we visit? How large a supply of pills can Dr. Lennard prescribe at once?

Sally was less taken. More hesitant, to her credit. She said, If he's ready to rejoin the world, he should prove it by holding a job for six months. Crawl before you walk. But it had been three, almost four years. That phone call from Columbia, an asterisk on the calendar. And I wanted another. Another date to mark—when he got well, when the avalanche revealed itself as something else. Benign.

In addition to which, I'd started to have—I shouldn't be writing this—secret inklings. That his life, broken husk, might be given over to the supraworldly. Maybe the torments he'd been suffering, the terrors and private panics, were his induction. One of my—not regrets, but compromises in bringing Thomas up in D.C. was the paucity of . . . that which couldn't be discussed on soccer sidelines over orange slices. Teachers, parents, very charming, wonderful—but living, fundamentally, between the forty-yard lines of George Will columns. Spirituality as the Montgomery Mall Christmas choir.

My own twentysomething crisis, thirty years earlier, had entailed a trip, not to India but to Thailand, this was just after the war—thatch hut by the Chao Praya, morning mist, an actual tiger (seen once, at a hundred feet, mini-fridge head lowered to a riverbank). This had been, for many years, the great adventure. I'd try to describe it at dinner parties, second bottle of red wine, Sally kicking me under the table. But there had been—under the influence of kratom and possible undiagnosed malaria—a vision one dawn in my hut. The moment—until Thomas was born—that I would have presented if aliens had descended, asked us to sliver up our pasts like cold cuts.

You must, it occurs to me—if you ventured into the Penn philosophy department at all—have read William James. More humane than his brother, better writer too. He gets to the end of *The Varieties of Religious Experience*—brilliant babbling encyclopedia of trances, conversions, shivers beneath crucifixes—and finally offers up the great unifying X between Christians and mystics and lotus-posed Japanese: "the 'more.'" The sap in the veins of all religion. The nagging feeling that outside the frame, or behind the canvas, there's . . . that which all the costumes and stories and nonsense can only gesture at.

I wondered if that's what Thomas had tasted, was seeking to taste. If—again, cursed vanity—the neighbors and ex-teachers who saw him in his Blockbuster uniform—no, no receipt, thank you—who played the parlor game of imagining what had gone wrong, if the joke might be on them. He could be great on a scale outside the stadium entirely. India.

I once saw a nature movie on PBS in which a group of wolves tore a coyote limb from limb. The camera may have cut away before the actual tearing, or I may have looked away, but what stuck with me was the look on the coyote's face at the moment when the pack closed in around him; *This,* he seemed to say, *is finally it. No more running. No more fear.* He looked almost awestruck by his own helplessness.

That was my feeling, that might very well have been my look, as I watched Manish come to the door.

I only learned afterward that even if I'd found Thomas earlier, it would have been too late. He'd been calling the Batras for weeks, leaving messages, telling them there was something they needed to know about the second car and the accident that killed their daughter. He'd walked from Delhi to Noida, sleeping on doorsteps, meditating under trees on median strips, spending the only money he had on pay phones. He must have mentioned the anniversary, although they might not have had as precise an idea of the accident's timing as we did. Anyway, I didn't know any of that; I just knew that I needed to do something and that I couldn't think of anything to do.

Manish was wearing a blue Georgetown sweatshirt and slippers; he was bald with square glasses and full lips. There were lights on in the house behind him. His expression was like the one people give telemarketers or Jehovah's Witnesses, a readiness to be bothered, but underneath you could see that he was agitated; he looked like someone who'd been waiting up.

"Excuse me," Thomas said, "are you Manish Batra?"

"I am," he said. He had the faintest dusting of a British-Indian accent.

"May we come in?" Thomas spoke as carefully as if he were laying dominoes in a row, his eyes almost closed with concentration. "I'm the one who's been calling. I would like to talk about Mira."

"Come in," Manish said, his voice shaking. We followed him into the living room, which seemed to be the kind of room that people don't actually use—perfectly fluffed cushions, arranged pillows, a lamp on a glass side table. The house was a single floor. Another man, who looked like Manish but younger and darker, hovered in the kitchen. I couldn't tell if the house was freezing or if this was something that was happening just in my body.

To the extent that a plan was shaping up in me, pressed there against the arm of the sofa, trying to stop my leg from shaking, it was: leave as soon as possible. Wait for Manish to look away or turn around, then grab Thomas and run. At the moment, though, I was finding it impossible to look up from my lap, which meant that I was staring at Thomas's tortoise-shell toenails. I kept smelling something, either Thomas or his clothes, that contained so many layers of BO and dirt and grease that it was almost beyond the smell of a person; it was the smell of an ecosystem. Grab him and run.

Manish said something in Hindi to the man in the kitchen that must have been "Bring them glasses of water," and then, sitting down in the chair opposite us, he said, "You are from Washington?"

"Yes," Thomas said.

"I did not know whether the calls were serious. My wife wanted me to stop answering."

The younger man, who must have been a son, stood in the doorway between the living room and the hallway, his arms crossed in front of him. On the wall behind Manish there was a long wooden mask, an animal with its tongue hanging out. The light in the room was flickering with the spinning of the fan blades.

"I didn't know Mira," Thomas said, his eyes fully closed, his back perfectly straight. "But I was there for the accident." He took a few long breaths through his nose, and I didn't know if he was going to say anything else.

"My friend's very sick," I said. "You can see, he's been homeless, he's been in the hospital, and I actually came here to—"

"I lived"—long breath—"on Macomb Street. I was only fifteen. I want to tell . . . I want to tell you that I was the one who did it."

"My friend really doesn't know what he's saying. He read about your daughter in the newspaper and he got obsessed and he started making things up. I'm so sorry that we've bothered you like this."

"There was"— long breath—"another car." He spoke exactly as if I weren't there. "There was no one driving it. That"—long breath—"was why Charles Lowe swerved."

"I'm so sorry, he doesn't know—"

"She was wearing a purple shirt"—long breath—"jeans and a purple shirt. Charles Lowe"—long breath—"was driving a green SUV."

In that moment I could see something happening in Manish's face as if he'd been stuck with a syringe: he'd been turning between the two of us, one skeletal and solemn, one fluid and apologetic, and he'd realized just then that the skeleton was the one telling the truth. Suddenly he was looking only at Thomas, and, although his expression hadn't changed, he'd started to cry; tears ran straight from the outer corners of his eyes.

"What are you telling me, please?"

Maybe that was my actual coyote-in-a-wolf-pack moment. Can you die of a desire not to be where you are? My ears for some reason felt in danger of combusting. There was nowhere I could safely look. I couldn't speak or move.

Thomas opened his eyes. The sentences he spoke (and his tone was steady, step after step on a tightrope) weren't so different from the ones that had been fermenting in me for the past decade, although they seemed to take an hour for him to get out. He'd been playing a game with his parents' car. He'd jumped out while it was moving. He'd panicked, and wept, and watched the news. He'd tried to live his life, but found that it wasn't possible. He knew he was beyond forgiving.

By this point the son was standing behind Manish's chair, with one hand on his father's shoulder. If anyone was going to kill us, I thought (and this did seem like more than a theoretical possibility), it was going to be the son; his jaw was clenched, his eyes were fixed and shrinking.

"And who are you?" the son said.

"I'm his friend."

"Were you there? Why are you in my house right now?"

Manish, taking off his glasses, waved his son off and made a strange, wincing face, almost as if he were about to laugh. He sat forward so that his knees were touching the edge of the coffee table.

"Do you know," he said, so quietly that I couldn't hear him and breathe at the same time, "do you know that my wife has not prayed, has not cooked Sunday dinner, for twelve years? That we have moved across the world, to not be on streets that we used to be on, to not see faces in parking lots and to wonder if they are classmates?"

Thomas laid his hands on his legs and lowered his head, and I thought: Is he getting ready to be killed? Is he about to pull a samurai sword out of the leg of his pants? Manish kept talking.

"Our life in Washington . . . we used to love Washington very much. When Mira was young she would lay her clothes on the floor, in the arrangement she was going to wear them. She counted the brushes of her hair. She would tease me for my belly, make me stop from going to Ben and Jerry's."

Amita must have heard something in her husband's voice; she appeared in the hallway; she was tiny, in an orange nightshirt, with plump bare feet and a gray braid to the bottom of her back. Her face looked as if all the blood, all the everything, had been drained out of it.

"When the phone call came," Manish said, "I was downstairs in the kitchen. Amita had never heard me scream that way. She thought I had burned myself. She came into the room, she saw my face, she fell to the floor. In the hospital there were so many machines I did not at first think Mira was in the bed. The doctor wanted to give me a shot, but I wouldn't let him."

"*Mumma,*" the son said to Amita, "go back to bed," then something low in Hindi, going over to her, putting his arm around her.

"Here we keep a nice house," Manish said. "You see the tomato garden, good family, nice friends. It is a puppet show. We wake up, go to work, go to sleep, the clock is the puppeteer. All the time we are in Washington. All the time we are trying not to say certain things." (The son had led Amita out of the room now; down a hallway I heard a door close.) "I did not believe, you know. I did not believe there was a second car. Amita did. She would say to me, '*He would not lie, I saw it in his face.*' I couldn't look at his face."

I must, without noticing it, have been moving farther away from Thomas on the couch, because I was almost sitting on the arm. Manish was silent now, not looking at either of us; he looked as if he were alone. I don't know if a minute passed or a half hour. I don't think I could have told you just then, listening to Thomas breathing and my watch ticking, a single thing that had happened in the past decade of my life. What should have happened immediately after the accident— prison, execution, vaporization—was going to happen now. Those years had been a rest between chords.

"I would like for you now," Manish said, "to leave my house." His eyes were on Thomas again. "You will think I must hate you, that I wish you harm, and if it were nine years, ten years ago, I would. But now I do not. I do not wish you happiness, but I see, I see in you, that you do not have it. I waited for your phone calls, for you to visit. I was very fearful; I thought there might be a great change. Now I don't know why. I am sorry. You must go."

He walked us to the front hall, past family pictures and a hanging rug. We'd been inside for forty minutes, the length of a nap, of a TV show. I don't think I've ever heard a sound like that front door locking behind us; it was like the bolt being thrown in a jail cell, but I couldn't tell if we were on the inside or the outside. The moon above the trees was enormous. The air smelled like asphalt.

There used to be these green glow sticks that we'd carry on Halloween (they were probably full of poison; we kept them by the hot dogs in the freezer), and to make them light up, you'd crack them, like breaking a bone. I felt like one of those lights now, but instead of light I was glowing with shame and horror and a feeling of not quite being in my body.

Thomas walked slowly down the middle of the road; I picked up my backpack from behind the bushes and stood there in the dark just watching him go. What was he thinking? Where was he going? I was in the middle of India, in the middle of the night, in more pain than I'd felt since dislocating my shoulder when I was eleven. I was seriously considering heading off in the opposite direction and never talking to him or thinking about him again. Treat him, treat everything to do with him, like a bad dream you wake up from in the middle of the night and tell yourself to forget.

But something in me, even then, was apparently clearer headed than that, or at least working toward some other goal. I caught up with him at the corner (the same corner where my auto-rickshaw had turned a few hours earlier), and I was about to say, "Wait," when I realized that he'd heard me coming up behind him and that he'd already spoken. His voice had been just as calm and strange as it was inside the house, so at first my brain took in the tone but missed the words; those came a second later. "You're a coward."

From: \<Thomas Pell\>

To: \<Adam Sanecki\>

Date: Sun, Jun 28, 2009 at 4:02 AM

Subject: re: (no subject)

. . . What I learned here I didn't come here to learn, it
was an accident, not an accident, it was done by invisible parts of me, my suffering, I thought in India it would
be better, it wasn't, now I couldn't talk, couldn't sleep, I
walked until my feet bled, didn't feel them, the particular
pain was not separable from the general pain, I wrote to
S and R, three sentences would take an hour, I would tell
them I was happy, I was working, not to worry, then back
in the street I would knock on doors, beg for food, look
for clear places to lie down, count hours like years of a jail
sentence, I knew I had made the final mistake, it was so
hot, I was lost, I thought, When does the body begin to
eat itself, please start with the brain, I would sometimes
think I'd become something else, a dog, a spider, I would
touch my body, it was still my body, it was as strange to
me as a farm tool, a broken machine, one day, I had been

sleeping, sleep was not a relief, it was worse, someone
found me, brought me to the center, carried me like a
corpse, I thought, The cemetery, the pyre, I need to wake
up so I can explain that I'm alive, why can't they hear me.
But I must have slept, I was inside a dark room, I heard
quiet music, bells, my head was on a pillow, I opened
my eyes and saw his face, he was on his seat, it was the
first thing I'd seen since leaving home that didn't scare
me. He didn't look at my clothes, my hair, I saw this in
his eyes, he was so calm, so kind, I wondered had I met
him before, he looked as if he knew me. Suddenly I was
trying to sit up, to speak, my lips felt thick as thumbs. I
wanted to say, saying it was the only thing I cared about,
I'm so glad I didn't die. I didn't know where the thought
had come from, I had forgotten the feeling of happiness, it
was like a word in another language, no sounds came out,
it was OK, he touched my hand, I understood, I needed to
learn what he knew, this was what would let me live, this
was what I'd been kept alive to do . . .

From: \<Sally Pell\>

To: \<Adam Sanecki\>

Date: Wed, Jul 22, 2009 at 9:36 PM

Subject: re: thank you

. . . One phrase that came to mean a lot to me was "out of the woods." When Thomas started working, and started seeing Dr. Lennard, and started talking about wanting to travel, I'd sometimes turn to Richard and ask, "Do you think we might be out of the woods?" (We never have to tell each other when we're talking about Thomas. It's the ongoing conversation for us, with occasional interruptions for what to make for dinner.)

I don't know why it was "out of the woods" in particular. I'm not sure I'd ever used the words before in my life. I think it might have gotten into my mind from disease movies, you know, the sorts of things you find yourself watching a bit of on TV, crying when the doctor finally tells Sally Field that the cancer's come back.

We were meeting with Dr. Lennard one day, Richard and I were, and he was explaining to us why he'd prescribed Thomas the medicines that he had, and how he thought a job could be a very good thing. And just before we stood up to leave, I found myself asking, just almost wriggling with hopefulness, "Do you suppose we might really be out of the woods?"

What a fool. I knew it as soon as it was out of my mouth. The look he gave me was a look he must have so much practice in giving. Just one parent who doesn't get it after another. I'll never forget what he said to me. His tone wasn't cruel—he was actually a very lovely man— but you could see that he wanted to be sure that there was no mistaking him either. "Mrs. Pell," he said, "with patients like Thomas, what we hope for is to manage the symptoms. Thinking in terms of cures is only, I'm afraid, going to lead to heartbreak. In other words, there are only woods—and we'll have to do the best in them we can."

So it turned out I'd get to spend a night at the Noida Radisson after all.

I led Thomas, without either of us saying another word, away from the Batras' street and down to a taxi stand where a line of auto-rickshaws sat waiting. We were like a couple walking away from a party at which they'd had a terrible fight; I had my hand between his shoulder blades, to make sure I didn't lose him, but there were quantities of shame and fury I needed to digest before I could interact with him any more directly than that.

We were in an auto-rickshaw speeding along the left lane of the empty highway when he started to talk. "Did you come here on your own? Where are my parents? They know everything. They're trying to make me say it first. Have you talked to them?"

He sat perfectly upright, but he didn't sound agitated; his voice was like someone reading off street signs. "Are you still having girl problems? Where do you live? I know you told me but I forget things. I forget everything I don't write down. I shouldn't have said you're a coward. I don't know if you really are. You might just be deluded."

I hadn't said a word to him yet, and at that point I didn't know if I'd speak to him at all. My feelings, my thoughts: I figured I could keep them all on hold until Thomas and I were strapped into our seats on a direct flight to Dulles. At that moment I was trying to think just about getting us from the auto-rickshaw to the hotel, from the hotel to the Delhi airport, and from the airport to D.C. Maybe he'd put up a fight, maybe he'd shout to everyone we met that I was a coward and a traitor, but I was going to get Thomas home safe and more or less sound if it meant stuffing him in a burlap sack. I could fail in every conceivable way but not in this.

The auto-rickshaw let us out under a massive glass hotel awning (there were palm trees next to the driveway), and even though it was half past one in the morning, and even though we looked like we'd just crawled out from a pile of construction rubble, a bellhop in a red uniform raced out to meet us and to carry our backpacks into the lobby ("Please, sir, good evening, good evening"). I hadn't felt actual goose bump–causing air-conditioning since leaving D.C. There were two-foot vases with flowers the size of umbrellas. There was, for some reason, a Montblanc store and a giant framed picture of Bill Clinton.

You can't believe how normal an interaction it's possible to have at even the least normal moments of your life. The woman behind the front desk (she was younger than me, wearing a dark blue blazer and a neck scarf) smiled and tapped at her computer. We'd like a room, please. Yes, I'll be paying with a MasterCard. No, we don't need an executive suite. Thank you, that would be wonderful. Oh, breakfast is included? OK, excellent, thank you so much.

And up we went.

I think now, in retrospect, that something in Thomas's manner, his detachment, the way he seemed not really to notice where he was, should have tipped me off. He didn't ask why we were checking in to a hotel, or where we were going next. I'd heard somewhere that murderers get like that, after they've committed their crimes; the terrible thing is done and now everything else is epilogue. Maybe that's what I imagined was happening with Thomas. He'd confessed, he'd done the thing he'd come all the way to India to do, and now he didn't mind being treated as a piece of human luggage.

"What's your mom doing?" he said. "Does she still yell at Frank? She loved you. I'm not sure if my parents did. Love me, I mean. They definitely loved you. I think you were a much more natural fit."

Our room was fancy, in the thick-carpeted, glossy-tabled way of these places. Our window, which didn't open, looked over a covered-up lap pool and, beyond that, a traffic circle.

"Do you remember that weekend when we went to a craft fair with my parents? Was that in Baltimore? I remember we stayed at the Hyatt. It was the first time I'd ever stayed in a hotel room separate from theirs. You called the front desk and pretended the toilet was overflowing. We tried to stay up all night."

The first thing I said, and I said it more to the room than to him, was: "I'm gonna shower."

I left the bathroom door cracked open, so I could keep an eye on Thomas in the mirror; he was sitting cross-legged on his bed, his eyes closed, his hands resting palms up on his knees. This was the first scalding, high-pressure water that I'd felt in I didn't know how long. I scrubbed my entire body, rinsed off, then scrubbed my entire body again. Maybe I was the one feeling like a murderer. Every minute or two a memory from the Batras' would pierce me like a needle hidden in the washcloth. *She counted the brushes of her hair. She would tease me for my belly.* Enough. No. I couldn't, I told myself, have made it more than a decade if what had happened, what I'd done, was actually as awful as it just then seemed. Get through tonight, get through tomorrow, sleep; then worry about bigger things. Or maybe don't.

"You should shower," I said, walking out into the room wrapped in towels, pulling back on my only pair of boxers.

"No, thank you."

"Get in the shower."

"All right."

What I needed, I'd decided, other than to get the two of us home, was to make sure that his truth-telling mission was over. Which is to say: I needed to confirm that Thomas didn't intend to tell his parents anything about what had happened here. I didn't think he would (his parents still seemed to exist for him in a reality-distortion field), but I needed to be sure, and my need to be sure was like a bad stomachache. Or I had a bad stomachache, which was somehow tangled up with my need to be sure in a way that was making the feeling even more intolerable than it would have been on its own.

I sat down on the bed and turned on the BBC, my first TV since home. Someone, or multiple someones, was renewing an economic treaty in East Asia. Someone else was no longer considering running for prime minister of Portugal. Then there were crowds and crushed metal and police barricades; apparently there had been a train accident in Jaipur. A correspondent stood outside the hospital.

"They've been counting the dead all night, after the most horrific accident in a year that's had no shortage . . ."

I must have fallen asleep for a second, or a wire in my brain must have misfired. Suddenly there were tears in my eyes, and for some reason I was standing up. At first I thought I'd heard Thomas leaving, but he was still in the shower; the bathroom door was still closed. "And now, a look at the world markets," the anchor said, and I noticed that I was squeezing the remote so hard that my fingertips were red.

The world markets were doing very poorly.

The human rights people who say that sleeplessness really is a kind of torture, not to be treated any less seriously than waterboarding or starvation, are right. The question of when I'd last gotten a significant quantity of sleep was beyond my computing abilities at that moment, but it had been a couple of days, at least. Pathways in me were corroding. Brain surfaces were drying out like old oranges. There's a level of exhaustion at which you could sleep through your own execution and I seemed, maybe because of a Pavlovian response to touching the bed, to have arrived there all at once.

The next thing I remember is lying on my bed, too tired, or too confused, to figure out how to get under anything other than the top comforter. The TV was off now. And I remember seeing Thomas on his bed, not asleep, lying on his back. Every now and then he'd say something, but I could only sort of mentally bat at whatever he'd said, like a balloon passing overhead.

"The strangest part of this," he said, "has been that I keep forgetting who I am. That's one way he said you know you're ready. Someone asked me my name and I had to stop and think."

And: "Do you remember when we used to sit out in the driveway and pretend to fight when cars passed?"

And: "The only time I ever really saw my dad so mad that I was scared was when I asked him what it felt like to kill someone."

And, some time later: "Do you think he forgave us? I didn't expect him to, but I think there has to be peace in knowing. What do you think?"

All throughout this, the lights in the room were blazing. Really, they were the brightest lights I'd ever seen. Could they possibly have been like that when we'd come in? It was like trying to sleep inside a bonfire. I spent minutes, like someone crawling toward a doorway, summoning the energy to beg Thomas to get up and turn them off. And then, even though I'm fairly sure I didn't say anything, he did. Or they went off, anyway. Oh, it was so sweet, like having my brain bathed in the most delicious blue-black liquor. All is coolness.

When I woke up again, hours had passed; I was under all the sheets now, sweating copiously, and the light from the alarm clock on the table between our beds had turned the whole room the pale green of night-vision goggles. Thomas was asleep, still in the hotel robe, holding his fists at his chest. I looked at his face, really looked at it, for the first time since I'd seen him. His beard was so long that it hung off the bottom of the pillow. His lips were gathered into the same thoughtful pucker that he'd worn to sleep when he was twelve years old. His legs, crossed at the ankles, were as thin as wrists. It was 4:09 in the morning, and my brain still shrieked for sleep but the rest of me was insistently awake, as if I'd missed a test or a flight. And then I knew: I needed to email Richard and Sally; this would probably be my last chance to sneak away from Thomas.

Unfolding the bedsheets as carefully as layers of phyllo dough, then pulling on my shorts, my eyes fixed the whole time on Thomas, I slipped out into the hall. Hotel lobbies in the middle of the night are like wax museums: so much uninhabited brightness and cheer. The business center, down the same hallway as the bathrooms, was somehow five degrees colder than the lobby; I sat at the computer all folded over on myself, my leg hairs trembling. The Internet's another wax museum. *Looks Like You're Signing In from a New Computer! Would You Mind Answering a Few Quick Security Questions?*

I typed the email with cold blue fingers, my brain lowering a curtain every time I blinked.

From: <Adam Sanecki>
To: <Richard Pell>; <Sally Pell>
Subject: I'm with Thomas
Date: Fri, Aug 7, 2009 at 4:16 AM

Richard and Sally—

I'm writing this from a fancy hotel in a suburb outside Delhi, and I just wanted to tell you that I've got Thomas. He's safe and asleep upstairs. My plan is to put us on a bus back to Delhi tomorrow and then to put us on the soonest possible flight back to D.C. I'll explain everything

about finding him when I have more time (I haven't slept
in a couple of days), but the short version is that some
friends pointed me toward him and that he'd managed to
wander a good ways out of the city. For now I just want to
say that he seems healthy, he's coherent, he knows where
he is. He seems still weird on the subject of you guys,
potentially, so I think the safest thing is for me not to tell
him I've been in touch with you. In any event, hopefully
we're going to be back home as fast as Continental can
carry us.

With lots of love,

Adam

Back upstairs I dipped the key card in the door as quietly
as I could; of course I knew Thomas would be there, but still,
when I saw his back, saw that he hadn't moved, I gave a silent
nod of thanks. How long had it been since he'd slept on an
actual bed, let alone a bed with a Serta-certified pillow-top
mattress and a down comforter?

And now I could give in to sleep too. Now I could relish
climbing into bed, nestling into the stack of pillows, sealing
the comforter around my neck, like a gourmand tucking into a
five-course meal. It was 4:24. *The next bed I lie down on will be in
America. The land of tap water and well-paved streets and as much
Internet/TV/alcohol as I decide to prescribe myself.* Sometimes in
bed, at moments of especially conscious tiredness, it feels like
you can steer yourself into a particular dream region, like
guiding a spaceship into a wormhole. No highways, please.
Let's dream about a forest, I told myself. It's warmly raining and there are soft-furred animals nuzzling you and all the
rocks are really trampolines. I dreamed and dreamed, slept
and slept; I gorged on sleep, rolled around in it, drank it
until I was full. Every now and then, to mark my progress, I
checked the clock: 5:39, 6:50, 7:28. I checked Thomas too; he
was as still as if he'd been unplugged. Maybe this was a sleep-

ing technique that Guruji had taught him. Maybe I'd have to carry him to the airport like a dad with a baby strapped to his chest.

When I opened my eyes at 8:45, my first thought was that I'd forgotten about all the states of being that don't include a headache. For a minute I just lay there in bed not hurting, studying the light fixture in the ceiling, letting the sunlight from between the curtains fall across my chest. You can somehow tell, just from the pitch of the silence, when it's snowed while you were asleep; I think the same organ can tell you whether there are other people in a room with you; I think that may have been why I gave myself a few extra seconds before I rolled onto my side, a few last breaths in which it wouldn't be confirmed:

Thomas's bed was empty.

I didn't panic. I called out, "Thomas?" and walked over to the bathroom. I knocked; maybe he was taking another shower. Nothing—empty. Maybe I'd just overlooked him in all those pillows and sheets. I pushed aside the hard, fabric-covered pillows on his bed, as if he might be hiding between them. I scoured the bedside table, and then the floor on either side of the bedside table, for a note he might have left: *Just gone for a walk, back in a few*. Nothing, nothing. I'd just thrown back the curtains, as if it weren't a person I was looking for but an earring, when I realized I was being ridiculous. Of course I knew where he was: breakfast. His body, with its scooped-out cheeks and countable ribs, must have craved food the way mine had craved sleep. I'd find him downstairs, planted behind a pair of buffet plates heaped with eggs and fruit and waffles.

Elevators are such a terrible form of transport when you really want to get somewhere. I rushed past the baffled hostess (who was, I was fairly sure, the same woman who'd checked us in the night before) and did a quick lap around the dining room. Purple paisley carpet, mirrors, white tablecloths. White families, Indian families, a group of women all reading from different guidebooks.

"Excuse me, did someone named Thomas Pell come down here and eat, do you know? Room 8021?"

"I'm sorry, sir?"

"Did a man from room 8021 come down here already? Would you mind checking?"

"I'm sorry. Would you like to sit for breakfast, sir?"

I hurried back through the lobby and out into the driveway, where it was already as hot as the middle of the afternoon. I ran past the line of cars and out to the sidewalk; I looked one way toward the traffic circle, the other way toward a high-rise, and realized that my running off in any direction would only make it much less likely that I'd find him.

You know what? I thought. *He must be in the room.* Maybe I somehow overlooked him, or maybe he was just out meditating in the hall. By the time I'd run up the stairs and reopened our door, I was feeling nearly hopeful. "You scared the shit out of me!" I'd tell him, and he'd nod at me like a benevolent tree being.

But the room was precisely as I'd left it. The bathroom door was open at just the same angle, the pillows on his bed were still where I'd thrown them. Now I was permitting myself, however slightly, to panic. I looked under both of our beds, even though these were the kinds of beds in which the "under" consists of a wooden box that goes all the way to the floor. I opened the shower curtain and looked in the tub not once but twice. I even, knowing it was insane as I did it, looked inside the minibar.

I spent the rest of the morning, and really the rest of the day, engaged in one of my least favorite (and lately most frequent) activities: anxious waiting. I sat on the bed, with the room phone beside me and the ringer turned up to maximum volume, watching more hours of cricket than I would ever have expected to consume. I ate all the dried apricots from the minibar, and then all the ginger snaps, and then all the Peanut M&M's, for a running total of $21.50. Every time the maids, or anyone else, went by in the hallway, I momentarily convinced myself that Thomas was about to open the door. How (really: *how*) was I going to tell his parents that I'd lost him again? I should have handcuffed myself to him. I should have slept with one hand clasping his beard.

I was aware, in a theoretical way, that some of my panic and grief at not knowing where he was (and by then I was sweating freely, shredding the packages in my hands into plastic strips) may have been borrowed emotion; which is to say, the fact that I hadn't really allowed myself to think or feel very much regarding the visit to the Batras the night before may have been causing me to feel more than I otherwise would have about what was happening today. Plus I was almost certainly still suffering from certain psychological effects of sleep deprivation. But still. Every thirty minutes or so I called the front desk to ask if anyone had been by to see me. Every hour I went down and checked my email (*YOU'VE FOUND HIM! Oh, Adam, we are dizzy with gratitude*). I kept standing up to look out the window, as if he might pop up swimming laps or sunbathing.

The sun had already started to set again (there's almost nothing more discouraging than the sunset on a day when you've hardly gone outside) when I decided, or admitted, that I needed finally to do the thing I'd spent the past few hours hoping and pretending I could avoid. I went back down to the business center, where I took my usual seat beside the preteen sibling British girls who'd spent the entire afternoon playing a game starring Dora the Explorer.

My teeth were chattering as I typed.

From: <Adam Sanecki>
To: <RBrough132@aol.com>
Date: Fri, Aug 7, 2009 at 7:06 PM

Raymond: I need you to tell me the location of the cave where Thomas was planning to go for his final retreat. I know you don't always respond to emails right away, and I know this is the sort of thing you'll say you have to confirm with Guruji, and I know he's sick . . . so I just want to be very clear. You need to respond to me as soon as you get this message, and you need to tell me, with absolutely no ambiguity, where to find him. I've just spent the day with a lawyer specializing in financial audits of religious institutions, and I hope you'll give me an excuse not to retain his services.

Thanks for your cooperation,

Adam Sanecki

· *Three* ·

———————

I should have (and under ordinary mental circumstances would have) known:

There was never a chance of Thomas not going to the cave. Running into me in Noida, being dragged to the hotel; all that, for him, was like having lint brushed from his costume as he headed toward the stage. He'd written himself directions, down to every last bus transfer and switchback. He'd made his way to the cave without a guide, with less struggle and complication than I would have thought possible for even the most capable local, let alone a half-crazy, starving foreigner. Maybe at some point in the past couple of years he'd developed a leather-soled native deftness; maybe he was just so desperate to get on with his enlightenment or his rebirth or whatever it was that it wouldn't have made a difference whether the cave was on a mountain or at the bottom of the ocean.

All of this is to say, I don't know exactly how or why, after the relative ease of getting there, he got into trouble. It may have been that by the time he found the cave, having traveled by train and bus for a day and then walked for a day after that, he was delirious with exhaustion. Or it may have been that, in the dark, he just got lost; maybe he got turned around and ended up crawling in deeper when he thought he was crawling out. Again: almost all of this is speculation.

About my own troubles, which started well before I found the cave, I can be much clearer.

Raymond responded to my email within a couple of hours, sounding somewhere between chastened and indignant; his note reminded me of the instructions for a scavenger hunt. First I needed to get to a city called Nainital (a surprisingly easy train ride, another set of town squares and city gates and auto-rickshaw drivers sleeping with newspapers shading their faces). And from there I needed to take a bus, which turned out to mean a couple of buses, thirtyish miles (most of them across a landscape so scrubby and bare that it made the whole problem of human overpopulation seem incomprehensible) to a tiny village in the Kumaon Valley near a city called Mukteshwar.

Throughout the trip I was performing a kind of triage on myself. To my running list of ailments I'd added a burning pain in the right side of my neck (which meant that to turn my head I needed to turn my entire body, like the Tin Man), a possibly infected blister on my left heel, and constipation paired with such vile gas that at each new occurrence I'd pause for a second, watery eyed, in miserable wonder that my body, or any body, was capable of such horrors. I did my best, on the bus, to linger at a level of sleep just deep enough to refresh me and just shallow enough so I wouldn't lose track of my bag. By four thirty that afternoon, when we pulled onto a dusty shoulder that was apparently as close as we were going to come to a bus station, I'd finished an entire liter of water, and I needed to pee so badly that the pain in my bladder had, in a weird sort of mercy, eclipsed every other sensation in my body.

The village ended up being not much more than a cluster of mud-brick houses. It was the sort of place that a long-sought mobster or Nazi might disappear to in order to reinvent himself as a bearded eccentric. In all four directions there were shaggy green mountains, carved in some places into terraced crops that looked like staircases. I didn't know if it was the off-season or if this was just a part of India that existed in a permanent state of heat-stunned emptiness. The town consisted of one main unpaved street, down which very few people walked, carrying much-reused plastic bags of things like tangled fishing line and dried reeds. All the dogs in town (there were at least a couple of dogs for every person) seemed to be either pregnant or sick or both. A group of boys kicked a plastic jug against a low, crumbling wall.

Raymond had told me to find a house belonging to someone named Akshay, so I spent my first hour in the village wandering up and down the road, farting toxically, peering stiffly into each of the dark little houses to see if I could find someone to talk to. In one building a man was sleeping on a cot with a woven blanket spread over his face. In another there seemed to be nothing but rusting engines. On the terrace in front of one house an old woman sat sorting dried beans on a towel while a shirtless little girl chased a rooster in circles around her.

"Akshay?" I said to her. "English? Akshay? I'm looking for Akshay's house?"

The woman had a daub of red on her forehead, and such deep wrinkles in her neck that their depths were a different color from the rest of her. She gave me an interested look, as if I were a squirrel that had happened to stop in front of her, but she didn't give any indication of understanding me; the girl now looked in danger of crying, possibly at the sight/ smell of me. I apologized vaguely and moved along. In the road, even though the sun was starting to go down, I kept getting that hand-over-a-grill feeling of imminent combustion. The rooster was now screaming in a way that the skin on the back of my neck interpreted, each time, as an emergency. I was starting to wonder if just this, the endless heat-stricken search, was my punishment. Maybe Thomas and I were like

Road Runner and Wile E. Coyote, only for us the chase wasn't funny, and we'd both end up as sun-bleached bones at the foot of a cactus.

At the uphill end of the road (the road literally just came to a stop, the dirt seeming to look out at the fields and the scrub and say, *You know what, forget it*) I found a general store, the first clearly open building I'd encountered. There was no door. The floor was covered in flattened cardboard boxes, and the shelves had so little (a tin of biscuits, a box of powdered soap) that the arrangements seemed more artistic than commercial. "English?" I said to the teenage girl who was leaning on the counter, making careful marks in a notebook that looked at least as old as she was. She shook her head. "Akshay?" I said. Again she shook her head, but after I'd bought a baby-food-sized jar of something that looked like mango jelly (she took a good two minutes to record our transaction in her notebook), she surprised me by leading me out of the store and walking a few steps ahead of me all the way down to the other end of the road, back to the terrace with the old woman and the little girl. She pointed to the house and made a sound that bore almost no resemblance to the way I'd been pronouncing Akshay; when I thanked her she just waggled her head and made a palms-up here-you-are gesture, as if she were introducing me to my brand-new washer/dryer.

By that point the little girl, who seemed to be five or six, had cheered up. She'd picked up a long stick with which, seemingly for my benefit, she kept poking a black dog that was trying to sleep, or die, against one of the house's outer walls. The girl would look at me, poke the dog, look at me, then burst into exaggerated, maybe teasing laughter, while her grandmother, now fiddling with a clothespin, shook her head disappointedly.

In his email Raymond had said that Guruji's disciples lived at Akshay's house, and that one of them would take me to the cave where Thomas was doing his retreat. My only question, by that point, was whether this was maliciously untrue or accidentally untrue. I was reconciled to resting somewhere to eat my jelly, then getting back on a bus and devoting what was left of my energy to finding and confronting Raymond. I was, in that moment, tired enough that I was ready to treat a seven-hour trip across India like a walk back from checking the mailbox.

But, mostly so as not to just stand there being silently stared at by the grandmother, I pulled Raymond's note from my pocket. Explain that you're *bhavishyat-savakabodhisatta,* he'd written. This may cause a bit of confusion but simply get on with it and don't flinch. I looked at the grandmother, cleared my throat, pointed at my chest, and pronounced each syllable with a hopeless little question mark attached, feeling very much like someone saying *"open sesame"* to a garage door. I could, for all I knew, have been telling her to please poison me; I could have been telling her I'd come from the city to eat her family. But she rose slowly to her feet (she turned out to be not much taller standing than sitting), bowed her head, and waved for me to follow her into the house. Open sesame. (She also shouted something at the little girl that sent her scrambling up the road as if someone were shooting at her feet.)

Inside she called something out toward the backyard, then got involved in making tea, which entailed lighting a burner with a long match and stuffing leaves into a rusty mesh ball. Either my eyes were now joining my list of misbehaving body parts, or this was the darkest habitation I'd ever seen. There were thick brown walls, low ceilings, windows as high and small as in a prison cell. In the main room, where she'd directed me to a chair against a wall, there were three beds (two of which were actually tables piled with blankets) and a scattering of plastic chairs. She set the teacup on the chair next to me, then stood expectantly with her hands together. I took a sip that amounted to not much more than a lip-touch. She made drink-up-drink-up gestures with her hands and grinned. I nodded and made what I hoped were appreciative noises.

At some point a man walked in from the backyard, tying the sash on his long shirt and pajama pants outfit; he was short and about the same age as the grandmother. "Welcome, welcome, so much welcome," he said, shaking my hand. "I am? Akki." He had the kind of barrel chest and thick white hair I associate with kings and billionaires. "My wife, who you are meeting? Shima. Our son? Very dead, very sadly dead. He is sorry you will not meet him. Stabbed. Very much bad business."

He called something toward another room, and a young woman shuffled in; she couldn't have much been much older than me, and she moved with the cautiousness of someone trying not to break through the surface of a frozen pond. Akki pressed her against his side. "The wife of my son. Gita. Very much beautiful. Very, very welcome to meet you." She didn't look very welcome to meet me. She hardly looked at me at all. She had gold bangles on her wrists and a daub of the same red on her forehead as the grandmother's. She nodded in my general direction, then hurried back to whatever room she'd come from.

"We are hearing not to be expecting you," Akki said. "This, you understand—" He gestured apologetically (I think) at the room, at the lack of special arrangements. I made a *pshaw* sort of noise and, in desperation, took a worrisomely sour gulp of tea.

"You are coming to us from miles and miles away," Akki said. "My English, I offer apologies. So many, many apologies." He moved his chair so he could sit facing me directly. "*Bhavishyat-savakabodhisatta,* very wonderful. Most wonderful. Telling me. You are a rich man? Important city man?"

No, no, a very unimportant man, I tried to explain. Unless you couldn't be a *bhavishyat-savakabodhisatta* without being an important man, in which case, yes, very important, extremely important, from the biggest city of all. I sipped more tea.

The grandmother, Shima, had gone off into the backyard and now she came back in carrying a chicken, which she set to work hacking apart on the tabletop; it took me a surprising number of minutes to connect what she was doing with the sudden absence of rooster crows.

Two things happened then, which, along with its getting dark outside, seemed to mark the tilting of the evening from one phase into another. First, the little girl came back from her errand, which had apparently been to buy two giant bottles of something label-less and golden. And second, as Shima went around the room lighting the lanterns, I began to notice a set of dark shapes gathering by the door where I'd come in. At first I counted three people, then four, then five, all lingering on the porch like carolers. "Do they want to come inside?" I said.

"They are hoping you give them numbers!" Akki said. "Many, many people, not very much educated. Someone say *savakabodhisatta,* they start to think of lottery. Start to think of magic." Then, to them, he said something that sounded like a grudging acknowledgment. One by one, bowing and cringing, they stepped inside and took their places against the wall. Were these the people who were supposed to lead me to the cave? They were mostly men, a few of them with mustaches; sometimes they whispered to each other, but mostly they just stood and watched as I served myself chicken bits and a purplish lentil stew. They looked as if they could have been waiting for a bus, or waiting to be called into a police lineup. By the time I'd finished my plate, which is to say picked at what meat I could discern in the half-dark, there were at least seven of them watching us.

"You are very much not feeling fear," Akki said. "Very much calm, very much preparing, many, many accomplishments. The final night for many, many things."

I made a noise of general agreement and wiped my hands against my shorts. The food was painfully, eye-reddeningly spicy, and the only way I could outrace the pain was by eating more and faster. Shima and Gita and the granddaughter had joined us, perched on chairs at a slight distance from the table;

Gita looked down at her lap and ate only with the finger-tips of her left hand, as birdlike as it was possible to be while eating stew without utensils; her daughter stood waiting to climb onto her lap. You'd think this might have been among the more awkward meals I'd ever eaten, but I was fairly well inured to awkwardness by that point, plus I'd resolved that a *bhavishyat-savakabodhisatta,* at least as I interpreted the role, wasn't really given to chattering.

Also, there was the alcohol. At some point it became impossible to keep track of how much I'd had, because Akki, like an overeager waiter, poured a refill (we drank from orange plastic mugs) every time I drank so much as an inch. *"Tulleho! Tulleho!"* If I had to guess I'd say it was whiskey, or maybe gin, but really what it tasted of most strongly was flammabil-ity. By the end of the meal I'd noticed that the doorways, for-merly very stable, were wobbling whenever I moved my head. One of the wall-lingerers, a pipe-cleaner-thin man in a white undershirt, seemed, each time I looked at him, to be mouth-ing a message to me, but I couldn't keep him still enough to decipher it. The possibility of vomiting appeared on the hori-zon, like a distant ship popping into view. I know I knocked over my mug at some point and I remember thinking, as the grandmother pressed a towel against the puddle and Akki apologized, *That's probably for the best.*

It was after dinner, in Akki's long whiskey-sipping gig-gling period, that I first noticed the singing coming from the backyard. It could have been going on all throughout dinner; I was having, by then, to keep a fairly vigilant watch on the table to keep the room from spinning. Akki had been in the middle of telling me a story about Gita's family (she'd gone to put her daughter to bed as soon as the meal was finished); she was, from what I understood, very lonely, much too shy to find a new father for her little daughter. There were other threads in the story too, things I couldn't quite follow, to do with cor-rupt judges, shady land deals. As I say, I wasn't at my best.

And anyway, the singing: it was a single voice, probably

female; going just by the melody I'd guess it was a song about waiting for a loved one to return from sea; it sounded like something you'd sing as you sat watching the plum blossoms wither. Either Akki noticed me noticing it or he noticed it himself. He stood up and lifted the lantern from the table; the men against the wall seemed to take this as their cue to huddle together by the door, as if they might need to run. "Come," Akki said. "Now we will see. They are as family to me. Very, very sad, when my son is dying. Lots of crying, much too much crying. They make happiness again."

The yard wasn't really so much a yard as it was a pen of dirt, leading out into an endless field. Except that I couldn't see details beyond Akki's lantern light, and what I could see, including the stars and the moon, seemed to be turning in a kaleidoscope. There's something about rural darkness, even or especially when you're drunk; it feels bottomless; it makes you feel like you're floating in the ocean. The lone voice had become a handful of voices now, a droning harmony, coming from somewhere that seemed to get farther away as we approached it. I tripped over a clod of broken-up ground and Akki put his arm around me, half affectionate, half stabilizing. He led me to the edge of the field, where there was a brick shed so basic it could have been drawn by a preschooler. The singing was coming directly from inside; if I'd lain my hands on the walls I would have felt a humming. Practically tiptoeing, Akki led me around to the shed's cutout door: *Look*.

And there they were, the disciples who'd brought Akki happiness after his son died, the people who were, I realized as soon as I saw them, my only hope of getting to the cave. Raymond had been telling the truth. They were all boys, and they couldn't, I didn't think, have been much older than thirteen or fourteen. They wore simple robes, something like orange togas, and had identically shaved heads. The singing seemed to come not so much from them as through them. One of them, the one I'd thought was a woman, would sing something that must have meant: *Must I, oh must I, wait for-*

ever? And the other three would answer: *Yes, yes, you must wait forever.*

They sat, the four of them, perfectly still, kneeling on the bare ground in what had been complete dark, singing with their heads tilted slightly toward the ground. It felt like coming upon a cluster of unicorns at a watering hole. In college, in a music appreciation class, the professor had once played us a recording of what she said was the last Italian castrato, this now ancient man, shriveled and broken, singing with the voice of an angelic little girl. That was, I'd always thought, the eeriest, most unworldly music I'd ever hear. Wrong.

Akki and I stood there until the song was done (I'm guessing it was at least a few minutes, because I had time to notice the rolled-up straw mats in the corner of the shed and the wood-framed photo, against the wall, of what must have been a much-younger Sri Prabhakara). Then, as soon as they were finished, all four boys, who I wouldn't have thought were aware of us, opened their eyes, turned to face us, to face me, and bowed until their foreheads were against the ground. I don't think the feeling of being wrongly prostrated to is something that most people get to, or have to, experience in their lives; I was lucky to be unsteady enough not to feel the full bizarreness of it.

They sat back upright and closed their eyes, and Akki, looking as if he'd just pulled off the world's most remarkable magic trick, led me staggering back toward the house. Was it possible that I smelled as strongly of alcohol as he did? Were those tears on his cheeks or was it sweat?

"Are they going to take me to the cave?" I said.

"Tomorrow, yes, yes, yes, tomorrow you will make *puja*. Now to resting. Now to sleep."

Someone had made up a bed for me, complete with a folded set of pajamas, while we were out in the backyard, and it looked, in that moment, as welcoming as a bath. It was right by the wall where we'd just eaten dinner, with a lantern tucked into the window nook above. The pajamas would have fit two of me, even with the drawstring pulled tight. I blew out the lantern and lay there listening to what sounded like a large animal just outside the back door, breathing and chewing. The room was warm but I wanted the protection of the blankets on me; either they or I or both of us smelled sweet and gamy. I tried, because exhaustion and the ability to fall asleep had parted company, to count the places I'd slept in India, but I kept losing track, having to double back. Under my mountain of blankets I turned onto one side and then the other, my back and then my front. I felt as if a plate-sized Alka-Seltzer were dissolving in my stomach.

There's no point, really, in ranking my nights according to their unpleasantness, but that one in Akki's dining room deserves some sort of special mention. Without getting too much into it, I'll just say that among the chicken's many other qualities, it cured me of my constipation. I spent a couple of pitch-black hours racing between my bed and the fields, squatting and praying in the dark, thinking that this time, finally, I had to have emptied myself of everything that could possibly have been inside me. Degradation, like awkwardness, can be gotten used to.

Also there was the half-dream I kept falling into, like a second bed, that I was still at the Batras', looking not for Thomas but for a doorway out, creeping around behind the furniture, trying not to be noticed.

And one other thing happened that night, which I'd say was another dream except that I was, by that point, past any hope of sleeping. It had to have been at least four in the morning, because the darkness outside had started to turn gray. I was lying there feeling empty and steamrollered, my eyes blurrily cracked open, when I noticed Gita standing next to me; my first thought was that she'd been sent to wake me up. No. She removed her sari like someone stepping out of a bathrobe and slid silently into bed beside me. I was so bewildered that I didn't say anything, didn't even move. Her skin was as smooth and cold as marble. She didn't acknowledge me.

She lay there as still as a mummy. And then, some number of airless minutes later, she was crying, a high, breathy sort of crying, as if she were suppressing a series of sneezes. "Gita?" I whispered. But as quickly and quietly as she'd gotten into the bed, she was out of it, clutching her clothes to her stomach and hurrying back out through the doorway.

The sun, when it came up, didn't so much rise as appear, like a blazing grapefruit, directly in the window. Shima was up, moving gingerly around the kitchen, rubbing what looked like ashes onto our dishes from the night before. She nodded *good morning* to me as I climbed out of bed. Akki was already in the field; the hacking sound I'd been hearing since dawn was him, working his way along between two rows, hunched and swinging a tool like the grim reaper's. The brick shed really wasn't so far from the house at all. Gita was in the corner of the field, looking conspicuously away from me, attaching something to a rhino-sized cow.

I'd just eaten breakfast, which is to say nibbled at a piece of round dry bread, when the monk came into the house from the backyard. He was, I was fairly sure, the lead singer from the night before. He was dark, with small eyes that made him look as if he were always just about to smile, and he had the thinnest of pubescent mustaches on his upper lip. He bowed at me again, staying on his feet this time. He was wearing his same robe and a pair of sandals that seemed to be made of tires and twine. He came up to about my chin. Akki, who'd followed the monk into the house, stood beaming in the doorway, sweating, dirt streaked across his forehead. He looked at the monk, looked at me, and apparently unable to contain himself any longer, he rushed over and pressed a pointer finger between my eyebrows, as if he were affixing a stamp to an envelope. He took me by the shoulders, beholding me, seeming seriously to consider kissing me. "We will be remembering you always."

A questioner from Germany asks: Is the proper teaching that we are to be mindful of every action always? Because it is often my experience that when I am trying to be most mindful, that is when my mind wanders the farthest.

Sri Prabhakara: Who is telling you, must be mindful? You are trying to control how is the state of your mind, of course you will find much suffering, much confusion. Do you see flowers? [*gestures toward altar*] Is flower thinking, being mindful, being mindful?

Q: Then the proper understanding pertains to effort? In making too much effort, I have been hindering myself?

P: In saying too much "I," have been hindering yourself. In coming to me, thinking there is "I" who will make you understand this and that. That is where hindering begins . . .

―――――――――

I should make clear that even under ideal circumstances, I'm no hiker. It makes my knees hurt, it makes my back sweat; I associate it with bad food, bad sleep, bad company. I've had terrible fights with girlfriends over my refusal to spend weekends camping. I've sulked my way through two-mile gravel-paved meanders.

So, as the monk and I set out through Akki's fields, between rows of something that looked like tobacco, then into a thicket of hilly woods, I kept repeating to myself: hiking is walking, hiking is walking. It was every bit as hot in the woods as it had been in the fields, and there were birds and bugs and frogs making trilly noises at every depth. There were more trees and tall grasses and bushes and vines than you could possibly count; the path looked days, or possibly hours, from being overgrown completely. You could see fallen trees turning back into mush almost in real time; there were mushrooms like orange tuning knobs along every trunk.

But I wasn't, at least for a while, doing too badly, and it took me a while to realize that this was because of how little I was carrying. On my summer camp Appalachian Trail hikes I'd carried, in addition to my idiotically bulky frame backpack, a sleeping bag, a Therm-a-Rest, a raincoat, a camp-ing chair, clothes, water, some share of the group's food, and probably a dozen other things I'm forgetting. You'd put down your backpack at the end of one of those days and feel, for a few minutes, that same weird weightless propulsion as when you step onto a moving walkway at the airport.

But now, thanks to my lack of foresight and to the relative emptiness of the village general store, I had:

(1) blue JanSport backpack, containing:

(4) miniature bags of Ritz-esque crackers

(2) liters of water

(1) red Mini Maglite, stocked with (2) ominously brandless AA batteries

(1) dirty sweatshirt

(1) box of not-very-adhesive Band-Aids

(1) composition notebook, and

(2) ballpoint pens courtesy of the Noida Radisson.

One reason the inadequacy of my provisions may not have been shriekingly obvious to me from the beginning was because, compared with my monk/guide, I was traveling with my own personal storage caravan. There may have been things I wasn't aware of tucked into the folds of his robe, but I'm fairly certain that all he had, as he scampered off ahead of me, were his sandals and, attached to a knotted string over his shoulder, a little enclosed bowl (which contained, I saw later, about half a meal's worth of lentils).

I hadn't learned his name; to myself I called him Ranjiv,

because he looked vaguely like a Ranjiv I'd gone to elementary school with. It seemed as unlikely that I'd learn his actual name, or that we'd have any sort of conversation, as that one of the birds cooing above me would fly down and ask how I was doing. He seemed to see me as an unusually large and helpless pink baby. He stopped to help me over a creek; he held back a thorny branch; he gestured for me to sit at a point when I happened to be feeling especially dire. I kept thinking I detected, behind the solicitousness, a kind of suppressed amusement in him. Did a fourteen-year-old Indian monk have friends? Go to school? Where was his family? Why had they let him get involved with Sri Prabhakara? He was, to me, an opaque little container of hypercompetence; his presence was the only thing that gave me any confidence that this hike wouldn't end with me eaten by a tiger or dead of heatstroke.

The hike divided into two basic phases. There was the *this-is-a-much-longer-hike-than-I'd-like-to-be-on-but-I'm-basically-OK* phase, which lasted from the time we left the house in the morning until sometime late that afternoon, when the path ended and we stopped to eat on a shale ledge overlooking what I'm pretty sure was Akki's village (Ranjiv wouldn't touch my crackers, and before he ate any of his lentils he insisted on bowing to me again). Up to that point my biggest immediate concerns were the heat and the blister on my heel, which had started leaving overlapping crusty bloodstains on the back of my sock and which was proving basically impossible to bandage. I couldn't ask, of course, but I'd decided, based on Ranjiv's calm and the fact that he didn't have even a canteen with him, that we couldn't have more than another hour or two to go; I thought, as we stood up and brushed ourselves off, that that might have been our farewell meal before we turned the corner and saw the cave. Instead, right after that commenced the *this-is-the-hardest-physical-thing-I've-ever-done-and-I-might-die* phase, which started when Ranjiv darted to a lookout at the top of a boulder, then gestured for me to follow him around to a clump of thorny vines that, so far as I could tell, we were the first people ever to disturb. This was a plateau at the top of the little mountain we'd been climbing all day, and it couldn't have been more than a half mile across, but it felt like crossing a continent. Why couldn't we go around the thorns? What we were doing felt, in terms of efficiency, like going from one room to the next by eating through the wall. I was wearing gym shorts and a T-shirt, so there was no shortage of skin for these thorns to find their way into. Except "thorns" may not be exactly right, because thorns you can snap off or, if they happen to get you, pluck out; these were more like hairs, stinging little cactus-fuzz hairs that covered the entire surfaces of these woody vines. For the seven hundredth time I wondered: How the hell had Thomas managed this? I'd seen tears come to his eyes when someone clipped his heels with a shopping cart.

To distract myself, and to keep from screaming, I decided that what I needed to do was play a game. Very few hiking games, it turns out, are designed to be played by one person. Not I Spy. Not that game where you say you're Alice and you're from Albuquerque and you like to eat apples. The only one I could think of how to play, unfortunately, was Sudden Death. Which is basically Twenty Questions, except that the answer always has to be someone who died unexpectedly. JFK. A passenger on the *Titanic.* Bambi's mother. So what I did, since of course I couldn't play in the traditional way, was to pick a person (Ritchie Valens) and then see how many questions it would have taken me to guess, if I hadn't already known.

At some point I discovered that the thorns hurt less on the backs of my arms than on the fronts.

Were you real?

And that the worst was getting them in the cheeks; that needed to be avoided if at all possible.

Were you famous?

And that if I stepped very high, while simultaneously

keeping my arms in boxer-protecting-his-face mode, I could let my knees take the worst of it.

Did you die in the last five years?

Maybe hopping; hopping might actually be better.

Was your death bloody?

We'd now made it to the shady side of the mountain, which, along with my sweat-soaked shirt, meant that I wasn't hot for the first time in days. But this seemed to be the hour of the late afternoon (and I would rather it have been fifteen degrees hotter) during which India's versions of horseflies come out. Or maybe it was something in our smells, our particular level of filthiness, that drew them. The only time I saw Ranjiv look anything other than totally composed was when he was slapping at a pair that were tag-teaming his neck. They were the size and weight of sugar cubes; they made frantic, helicopter-circling noises as they hovered by your ears; they stung with deep, epidural sorts of needles. I spent those entire couple of hours fondling the thought of their extinction like a prisoner plotting his revenge.

And they wouldn't, I don't think, have been quite so hard to deter except that I needed both hands to cling to the long grass as we made our way down the hillside. This hill seemed, and may even have been, slightly steeper than an average peaked rooftop. And this was a rooftop that happened to be covered in a shiny, *Honey, I Shrunk the Kids* sort of grass, all combed downward so as to facilitate maximum slippage. It's such an unfamiliar feeling, for someone who takes elevators and orders takeout and confines his exertion to softly padded weight machines, to be flexing your muscles *desperately,* and for hours. Something about the angle at which I was crouching kept making my left thigh seize up in little walnut clusters of pain. The fingers on both my hands were cut up and stinging where I'd been clutching at roots. My veins were hard as shoelaces. At one point, just when I thought I'd developed a reliable grab-and-shimmy method, a handful of roots gave way and I did a thing I'd never done before in waking life: I tumbled freely and helplessly. For what couldn't have been more than a couple of seconds I was without resistance, without a notion of where I'd end up. I came to a stop maybe fifteen feet below our little non-path, my feet higher than my head, my entire body sunk in wet grass. Something had torn a strip of skin from my thigh. I'd crushed everything in my backpack. This wasn't the first but it was probably the most serious of the moments in which I thought: *I give up.* I didn't know exactly what giving up would have entailed (lying there until horseflies had stung me to death; rolling down the hill until I was carried away in the river), but I couldn't imagine that it could be any worse than going on. If there had been anyone to tell me that it was all right, I would have cried; for the first time in India, maybe for the first time in years, I longed for the presence of my mom.

Ranjiv, looking down at me with alarm, gripped me by the shoulder straps, lifted me like a doll (this despite his weighing at least forty pounds less than me), and placed me on my feet. From that point on he never got more than a few feet ahead of me, and once we were past the steepest part of the hill, he insisted that we stop and rest. He refused to drink from my bottle; instead he made a little cup with the bottom of his robe and, squatting by the stream, drank for the first time that I'd seen all day.

His drinking, for reasons sensible or not, struck me as a very bad sign. As I say, I'd somehow taken his lack of water as an indication that this wasn't going to be a long hike, but now I began to fear (and this too felt familiar from the Appalachian Trail, watching as my counselors quietly conferred) that this might actually involve spending a night outdoors. It was beginning to get dark, different sets of birds and bugs were beginning to make themselves known, and something about the way Ranjiv was moving, his energy-conserving lope, signaled to me that this was a person who knew he had many miles and many hours to go. It's possible that my emotional state, like a fallen tree, was simply decomposing in hyper-speed, but I really, really didn't want this hike to include a night in the woods. I even pled to Ranjiv's back, in the hopes that my tone of voice might convey my meaning, "We're going to get there tonight, aren't we?" He just glanced back at me, concerned and a little irritated, as if I'd sneezed on his neck.

We weren't going to get there tonight. A couple of hours later (by which time it was nearly dark, and my legs had become numb little forward-motion machines) we came into a clearing, a dramatically pretty patch of fallen leaves enclosed by a creek and a wall of vine-swallowed trees, and Ranjiv pointed at the ground and made a sleeping-on-a-pillow gesture with his hands and head. Here we were. I sat down on the biggest rock I could find and took a glug of water that for some reason I had to work not to immediately throw up. I kept seeing little peripheral flickers in the underbrush, but it was probably just my eyes. I almost felt like laughing with unhappiness.

I was, of course, incredibly tired, but past a certain point tiredness stops registering primarily as a desire to be asleep. It was as if my body or brain had at some point in the past few days accepted that I was never again going to get adequate sleep, so it had constructed a jittery, pain-spiked simulation of wakefulness. It was to the real thing what a high school *Into the Woods* backdrop is to an actual forest.

But before we could sleep (and by now it was becoming truly dark, so I had to use my flashlight when I went to pee), Ranjiv had various things to do, little ceremonies. I didn't know if these were things he did every night, as a monk, or if these were things that had to do with me in particular. The whole time he kept the mildest, most blandly content expression on his face; he looked, here in the middle of the woods, alone with a white stranger he'd been told to revere, like someone unloading the dishwasher.

The first thing he needed to do, apparently, was to start a little fire. I'd never seen anyone do this before, outside of

Survivor, and he wasn't, surprisingly, particularly good at it. Or maybe the twigs he was using were just wet. Either way, he spent what seemed like twenty minutes gathering sticks and branches and leaves, then spinning one stick against another, on and on and on, until I thought maybe he wasn't trying to start a fire at all; maybe this was the whole ritual. But a string of gray smoke finally appeared, and then a flame about the size of the one in a votive candle. The whole time he was doing this, I was sitting on my rock, scraping thorns from my legs with the Pells' MasterCard. I wanted, for some reason, to stomp Ranjiv's fire out. I wanted to douse it in lighter fluid and burn every fly and plant and human on the mountain.

The dark, when you're in the middle of the woods, is so complete, and comes on so fast. I moved closer to the fire, now the size of a flame on a stove, and I just sat there, painfully cross-legged, a few feet from Ranjiv, for what seemed like an hour. My back hurt in every position I tried, so I settled on a hunch, with my elbows on my knees. If we'd been friends, if we'd spoken the same language, we would have been telling stories, complaining, tossing broken-off pieces of bark. As it was, we just sat. I tried toasting a cracker, which didn't improve its taste. Life must have been so terrifying, and so boring, when there was nothing to do at night other than sit around in the dark and stare at fires. I tried to remember the exact layout of everywhere I'd ever lived. I tried to remember what Thomas had had on the walls of his childhood bedroom. I kept thinking I heard voices on the water, rustling in the bushes; and (this is painful to think about now) I kept switching on my flashlight, as if the pale circle might just happen to catch whatever it was, and as if I might be able to do something about it.

At some point, just before he went to sleep, Ranjiv shifted around so he was facing me and launched into a set of prostrations that made last night's look disrespectful. He stretched all the way out into a push-up frozen just above the ground.

He cupped his hands at his forehead. He scooted forward on his knees and repeated it all closer to me.

"You don't have to do that," I muttered, waving my hands. "Really."

When he opened his mouth I thought he was actually going to respond to me, but instead he let out a single, mournful note (it *was* him leading the chanting), which he then repeated, at intervals, like a wolf baying at the moon, or like a beautiful human car alarm. I had goose bumps all over my legs, and only the thinnest tissue of sense kept me from shouting, "Stop! Stop! Please stop! This is insane!" Instead I closed my eyes and thought, *I don't know what I've done in my life to be where I am, or actually I do know, but please tell me I've paid my debts. Tell me I've done enough.*

It was time for bed.

Ranjiv swept dirt onto the fire, then curled up on the flat ground right where we'd been sitting. He tucked his knees toward his chest and pressed his hands together under his head (for him the sleeping gesture was apparently a literal reenactment). I curled up about five feet away, facing the opposite direction, and tried to understand that this was it, that these were the conditions under which I was going to spend the next however many hours of my life. I uncrumpled my sweatshirt and made a kind of blanket/neck pillow out of it. When I switched off my light, the darkness was almost perfect; there must have been cloud cover, because even the moon, which had been massive at Akki's, was nowhere. If I ever made it back to America, I decided, I'd go on a speaking tour, imploring people to think daily about the miracle of artificial light. Night was an enemy we'd defeated so thoroughly that we forgot we'd ever been fighting it. In the dark woods on the side of a mountain you're not the endpoint of all creation, you're just a small and not particularly capable mammal; you're a monkey curled in a tree, a wild dog with its nose buried in its paw.

It wasn't cold, except compared with the temperature that afternoon. The dirt smelled strongly of dirt. There was wind making the leaves rattle and bugs clicking and water hissing and so many more noises that I couldn't begin to identify: hoots and chitters and yelps and grunts. I'm not ashamed to say that I was crying, lightly. I was reverse-engineering civilization by the things that I missed. Sheets, pillows, heat, walls, and bug spray, good God, bug spray. Mosquitoes were working me over, draining me. One bite in particular, on the tendon on the back of my knee, had taken on a dark, hard, throbbing quality, as if my leg were trying to give birth to something. I covered it with the sleeve of my sweatshirt, and X'd the bite with my fingernail, which someone (it was Anna! my middle-aged mistress was somewhere on the planet right at that moment!) had told me helped dissipate the poison.

Every square inch of ground beneath me turned out to have qualities all its own. A little divot that took my shoulder as if it had been built for that purpose; a slant under my legs that eventually felt as steep as a ski slope. When dawn finally came, and I saw the plainness of where I'd been lying, the smallness and bareness of it, it felt like a trick. I brushed off my clothes and swished water around my mouth to get the taste out. It's much easier to get up, it turns out, when you've never really been asleep in the first place.

We must have been hiking again by five thirty or six; it was that kind of light, and there was a wetness on everything, a fresh-from-the-refrigerator chill. I ate half a packet of broken crackers, and I could feel my body burning them up, vaporizing them, like water droplets hitting a hot pan. The rest of our way was mostly downhill, through woods that were like pine but shaggier. I was seeing whitish question marks, little retinal floaters, everywhere I looked. I kept finding myself moved, almost to the point of tears, by the sight of Ranjiv; he was the little brother, or possibly the son, I never had and never would. Watching his shoulders and the back of his shaved head, I wanted to go and grab him, hug him, tell him to please go off and have a life, he could take my place in America. He was good and I wasn't, it seemed so clear, so indisputable. I wanted to find his parents and make them promise to take care of him; I wanted to give him real shoes, warm food, an apartment full of Ikea furniture and electronic crap. I wanted to lie down and die.

I didn't understand, at first, when we came to the mouth of the cave. It was less the crack-in-a-wall sort of cave that I'd been picturing than a kind of indoor amphitheater. We'd been following a steep path down, in front of a rock wall, and now here it was, only slightly obscured by trees, like the entrance to a small garage. I peered inside. There was a ceiling you'd have to jump to touch, wide walls, a slightly downward-slanting rock floor. I didn't notice until Ranjiv went over and bowed to it that there was a figure carved in the rock just to the left of the entrance; it was someone seated, holding up his right hand, just a few degrees more sophisticated than a stick figure. The cave wasn't exactly inviting, but here in the noonish light it didn't seem especially fearsome either; there didn't look like there was any point inside from which you wouldn't be able to see back to the entrance. I actually felt relieved.

My notion was that Ranjiv would lead us in, and that within fifteen minutes we'd either know we'd come to the wrong place, or we'd find Thomas perched somewhere just inside, like one of the bats I was now beginning to notice, shiny black faces poking out from the burned-English-muffin surface of the ceiling. Either way we'd be back in Akki's village by bedtime, or by tomorrow morning at the absolute latest, and I would have survived what had seemed like the least survivable thing I'd ever done.

By that point Ranjiv and I had developed a more or less reliable system of gestures and looks, but we'd mostly used it to express things along the lines of *Look out for where the path drops off* or *Let's rest until you've finished drinking*. This was more complicated.

First he made a gesture that was something like, *OK, this is it, you're welcome.*

I pointed inside the cave. Pointed to him and then to me.

He shook his head and repeated: *Thank you, no, our time together is done. You, alone, go inside.*

We wrestled over this basic point for a while. Was he saying he was afraid? That he wasn't allowed to go in? He looked, the longer we stood there, almost embarrassed for me, as if I were trying to insist that he accompany me into the bathroom.

I made a face, and may even have said out loud, "How the fuck am I supposed to go in there alone? And then how am I supposed to get back? Look where we are!"

At this point he dropped to his knees and started in on what I gathered were the final, farewell set of prostrations. I hoped very badly that I was misunderstanding him, but I didn't think so. When he finally stood up, he dusted off his robe, then looked at me, looked directly at me, and for the first time since we'd been together it wasn't the look a lowly soldier gives a general; it was more the look a man gives his house as it goes up in flames. But his gesture was unmistakable: *You stay here. Good-bye.*

I stood there watching his orange-robed back as he bobbed off up the path, not looking back, and then as he passed around the corner and out of sight. I felt like a dog being abandoned by the side of the road. There was an orbit of gnats around my head. I felt fear unfolding in me, expanding to fill my chest; I knew I should run after him, and kept feeling flickers of almost doing it, like someone at the edge of a diving board, but then it was too late, and I was standing by the cave mouth alone. The sun was making the ground steam, and a woodpecker was drilling away up high in a dead tree. I took a deep breath and, for the first time in my life, brought my hands together in prayer at my forehead. I turned and walked into the cave.

Q: It seems like everything's good, very peaceful, when I'm here, but then as soon as I get home, around my family, I feel old patterns coming back. How do I keep from getting caught up in my old issues whenever I'm living my "real" life?

P: Prior to meeting your family, prior even to being conceived, you were somewhere, yes? Or did you come into creation from nothing? To return to that prior state, that is how you will be free in all of life.

Q: I get that as an intellectual idea, but to really experience it sometimes, especially when I'm away from the center . . .

P: Center is in imagination. Family is in imagination.

Q: But it's hard, because my family doesn't believe any of the same things that I do. Like if they heard what you were saying now, and saw me listening to it, they'd think I was out of my mind. [*laughter*]

P: Does family believe that when an object drops, it falls to the earth, or does it float away into the sky? Unless they believe, is there no more physical science, no more gravity? Does your mother control seven heavens? Must I make *puja* to her? . . .

―――――――

Among the many impressions that I didn't know whether to trust as I started into the cave: a breeze, like the wind off the ocean in winter, coming from somewhere in the depths. Was that possible?

I called out, tentatively at first, "Thomas? Thomas?" I got nothing back, except an echoey fullness and dripping. The ground slanted down sharply enough that I had to walk with my feet sideways, as if I were easing along on skis. All the stone (and everything was stone) was wet, a from-within wet- ness, as if the walls were sweating, clammily. The ground was broken up in places, piled into rubble heaps. I probably didn't need my flashlight yet, but I thought about stopping to put on my sweatshirt. The entrance, when I looked back, was a bright yellow parallelogram.

I'd been in a cave before, as a kid, at the same camp in Virginia that had turned me against hiking. I remembered it mainly as hunch-walking down a tunnel behind a boy named Daniel who wore the same Alice in Chains T-shirt every day for three weeks. And I remember not being afraid. I was lonely and cold and, since my being at camp was one of my mom's attempts to have me make friends with people other than Thomas, resentful of just about everything I experienced. But I wasn't scared, and that, as much as anything, gave me hope that this too would be tolerable. I was having to stoop now (the floor and the ceiling were converging, as if I were walking toward the corner of an attic), and it was just about dark enough to turn on my flashlight, but still: *I'm not afraid of caves.*

"Thom-as? Oh, Thom-as?" By that point I was calling out to him mostly as a kind of verbal cane tapping. My attention was almost entirely on my body (the floor had gotten steep enough that I'd started scooting on my butt), but there were things I couldn't help noticing: that the walls were smeared with white; that there were puddles so still they could have been mirrors; that the bats (and there were bats everywhere I shone my light) were making a faint, collective chittering, like mice in the walls. I was talking to myself now, in addition to calling out to Thomas, a mix of encouraging babble (". . . all right now, just right down here and careful, careful . . .") and a kind of free-form cursing. Not only did it seem impossible that Thomas was in here, it seemed impossible that anyone had been in here. I imagined bears. I imagined cavemen frozen in amber (how had I never really heard the *cave* in *caveman*?). I clenched the flashlight like a cigar between my teeth.

It was around this point that I began to think, with a snowballing certainty, that this had all been an elaborate plot of Guruji and Raymond's to kill me. I imagined I could hear boulders being rolled back in front of the entrance; I saw my beloved Ranjiv reporting guiltily to Raymond that he'd seen me go in. The terrible perfection of it sent a chill through me like an ice-water IV. I couldn't turn back, couldn't leave Thomas (or couldn't leave without being sure I hadn't left Thomas), but I was in less and less doubt: this was what they did, they entrapped American people, cleaned out their bank accounts, stole their identities, told their families they'd gone missing and to please send money for recovery of the body.

"Ranjiv?" I shouted, idiotically. "Thomas?" I was a moron, a clueless foreigner; the nightly news would do a couple of stories ("Sad news from India tonight . . ."), accompanied by an incongruously smiling photo sent in by my mom. Was Thomas part of the scheme, or was he another of its victims? There was no one, just then, I wasn't ready to suspect, no one that seemed to me free of a hint of murderousness. The Batras could have been in on it. My stepdad. The girl who'd sold me water at the village store. The word *motherfuckers* had now come into heavy rotation in my curse-stream.

At some point maybe a hundred feet in, the cave, or what I could see of it, narrowed dramatically. There was rubble and water around me, but the enterable part, now, was not much bigger than the space under a table. Carved on a big rock next to this tunnel entrance was another of the little sitting figures from outside. I'd thought that what I'd done already counted as searching the cave, but apparently to that point I'd only been milling around the lobby. So in I went. There are so few occasions for crawling in an adult's life, I felt like I'd almost forgotten the mechanics of it. Palm, palm, knee, knee, palm, palm, knee, knee. It reminded me of crawling through the blue whale's veins at the Natural History Museum. When had that been? The echoing breathing, the feeling of tininess. *I am not afraid of caves.* After fifty or so feet the tunnel took a turn, and to go on (I was now officially to the point where going on was easier than going back), I had to do a pull-up onto a little ledge, which I didn't realize until I was back on all fours held a pool of water almost a foot deep. "Oh, Thomas? Thomas? Can you hear me? I hate you very much, Thomas. You're a motherfucking idiot, Thomas. Can you hear me, you fucking moron? I'm about to leave you." My knees and shins and hands were now soaked and freezing; I pulled on my sweatshirt, but that seemed only to make me heavier, not warmer. To do a U-turn now would have entailed scraping the top of my head on the wall. Only by making certain promises to myself could I keep from panicking completely: *If it gets any*

*narrower, I'll turn around. If it gets to where I'm not absolutely cer-
tain which direction the entrance is, I'll turn around.* "I hate you
so fucking much, Thomas, I really do. I'm going to go home
and I'm going to be clean and happy and you're going to be
fucking dead here, and it isn't going to be my fault. Are you
happy now? Are you purified?"

The tunnel did get narrower, and I didn't turn around.
A part of me must have known that I wasn't the only person
in there; or maybe it was just that by then I was so miserable and confused that dying seemed like a kind of mercy.
The ceiling of the tunnel lowered and lowered until the space
between the ceiling and the floor, the space for me, was not
much taller than my lying-flat body. Geology too seemed to
be in on the conspiracy. I took off my backpack and held it
under my armpit like a football. Each time I inhaled deeply
(and I was taking wide-mouthed, noisy breaths around the
light between my teeth) I felt the ceiling touch the back of
my shirt. My teeth were chattering. My head was sideways,
and I was advancing by sliding myself forward on my palms.
You'll turn around in ten seconds. Twenty seconds. Thirty. Everything looked like it had been painted in red and black; was my
light getting dimmer or was that my eyes? The sound in the
cave, something like running water, had gotten louder now,
but I wasn't at all certain that it wasn't just my blood. Would
mine count as a sudden death? *Were you real? Were you alone
when you died? Were you older than forty?* "I'm sorry, I'm sorry. I
hate you. I'm sorry."

The tunnel had finally opened up again, letting me rise
back up onto my knees, when I first really thought I heard
a voice. I was on all fours, hanging my head, gasping, and
I knew, if there had ever been a moment in my life when I
was going to hallucinate, this would have been it. I wouldn't
have been surprised to hear angels singing. I wouldn't have
been surprised to hear Mira Batra screaming. But what I did
hear, or what I thought I heard, was someone saying, "Help!
Help! Help!" Part of what made me think I might not actu-

ally be hearing it was that the voice seemed to be coming from far away, and from a place somehow *beneath* the ground I was kneeling on, where it didn't seem possible for anyone to be.

I called out, for the thousandth time, "Hello? Thomas? Hello?" Nothing. Or maybe something, but too faint to hear. You can hear voices in drips, in cave breaths, just the way you can hear music in airplane roars. I drank water, my first sip in an hour or two, and blew grit from my nose into my hand; the smell of wet, cold rock suddenly became much sharper. I slumped back against a wall, to keep my legs from freezing up. My knees were purple and pruny. My right sock was red with either blood or dirt. I was doing, and had apparently been doing, something between crying and whimpering. The tunnel went on, but I'd decided, or discovered, that I wasn't capable of following it. It wasn't that I didn't know which way the entrance was, but I could feel my sense of orientation wavering, going in and out like a radio signal, and I knew it would only get worse.

There was, I noticed when I went to wipe my hand, a puddle at the place where the wall met the floor, and there were drops falling into the center of it: *pock, pock, pock, pock.*

If I die here, I thought, *that'll be the last thing I hear.* What I didn't think right away, and again, I blame my mental state, was: *Where is the dripping coming from?* When I followed the shine on the ceiling with my light, I came to a crack right over my head, not much bigger than a pebble. I didn't touch it, for fear of bringing the tunnel rubbling down on me, but it was that crack that gave me the idea, at a moment when I didn't think I was capable of ideas: there was more to the cave than this tunnel I was in. If there could be water above me, there could be tunnels below me. I don't know if this was even coherent thinking, but it was my thinking. There could be an actual voice.

I don't know how long I spent scrabbling along with my ear to the ground (time was one of the many senses that had gone wobbly), but it was long enough for me to be sure that the voice was not just an echo, and that it was coming from somewhere below the part of my little chamber closest to where the tunnel continued. "Hold on! I'm coming! Wait!" So I did go on, now having to do a kind of military crawl on my elbows; by that point I was like a dog in the last frenzied stretch of a hunt.

It wasn't until I came around a little bend that the voice suddenly became much clearer, and that I understood just how far down it was coming from. "Hello?" I called. "Hello?" And as I lay there, a trembling antenna, there was finally a moment of quiet, a pause in both of our yelling, in which I knew that I'd found Thomas and Thomas knew that someone had come for him; it gave me goose bumps on the inside of my skin.

The tunnel dropped off into what I thought at first was just a kind of pothole (if I'd had my light off I might have slid in headfirst), but what turned out to be something much deeper than that; it was as if I'd been crawling along in an air-conditioning duct and had suddenly come upon an elevator shaft.

"Help! Help! Help!"

"Thomas? I'm here. It's Adam."

"Help! Oh God, help."

I was lying on my stomach, peering over the edge of the pit, struggling to find him with my light; the beam was barely strong enough to shine as deep as he was, and when I did finally find him, it was only his face, only the pale stretch of his forehead and cheeks, that showed up in all that dark. My heart was beating so hard that I thought I might faint or die before I'd even gotten to him.

"I fell," he said. "I hurt my leg. I'm so thirsty. Please. Help."

He didn't sound anything like the Thomas who'd been rambling to me in the hotel; terror had sharpened his voice and raised its pitch. He must have been twenty or twenty-five feet below me. From what I could tell his pit was about the diameter of a well.

"Thomas? I'm going to come get you."

"Yes. Yes. Please. Help. I need water. My light broke. I don't have anything."

"I just need to get down to you."

"OK. Yes. Please."

Again, I don't know how long I lay there thinking of what to do, listening to the cave breathe and to my heart thud, staring down into the dark, but at some point the thought arrived in my mind, as if it had been spoken by another voice, one at an even greater depth than Thomas's: *You need to leave.* And as soon as it had been spoken, a chorus of voices materialized to bolster it. How could I possibly get down to him without getting hurt myself? And how, if I did get down to him, would we possibly make it back up? I could tear up my sweatshirt and try to make a rope of it, but that would only reach a few feet, and it would never support a person, let alone two people, even if I could find something to attach it to. I could hurry back to the entrance of the cave and try to find someone to come back with me, but I'd never find anyone, and by the time I made it out and made it back, he'd probably have died.

"Don't worry," I said. "I'm coming."

But my secret had taken hold of me: I was going to leave him there. I wouldn't die for him. No one would want me to. Even he wouldn't want me to, if he were thinking clearly. Have you ever walked out of a room where a baby's crying? I had that kind of charge running through me, the guilt and the anticipated relief. *I'll never tell anyone that I heard him. I'll sneak off, he'll call for me, he'll suffer and I'll suffer, it will be the hardest thing I've ever done, but it will be right. It will be horrible but it will be right.*

One of the very few benefits of having caused someone's death before is that you have a nonimaginary sense of just how much it weighs emotionally. You understand what it would do to you to cause another. I can't pretend to know how much of it was that, as opposed to feeling for Thomas, or even the latent suicidalism that seemed to have been pushing at my back since before I left for India, but I just know that at some point I was telling Thomas I was coming for him and lying, and then that I was saying it and telling the truth. And that not more than ten minutes after finding him I was making my way down to him, starting to make my way down to him, via one of the strangest physical maneuvers of my life. Your body knows a huge amount more than you do about how to get along in the world.

I lowered myself into the shaft, bracing myself with the flat of my back against one wall and the soles of my feet against the other, as if I were trying to hold the walls apart. My backpack was hanging against my chest. Inch by inch, I shuffled my feet, shimmied my back, and moved down into the depths at the speed of an inchworm. My light was still in my mouth. If the walls had suddenly broadened out at any point, I might have plummeted, I might have landed directly on Thomas, but I proceeded so slowly that I could feel the walls' every bump and indent. I was concentrating so hard that there wasn't even room in me to be afraid, really. My plan, or "plan," was to give Thomas my water, and then for the two of us to climb out very much the way I was climbing in, like a pair of Santa Clauses shimmying our way up a chimney. Or maybe his little chamber would connect with another tunnel that would take us back to the main part of the cave. Or maybe he'd stand on my shoulders and jump.

I could hear him closer and closer now. When I came to where I could finally see a patch of ground clearly between my knees, I lowered my legs and let myself drop; it was like hopping off a wall, that little jolt in the feet and ankles. Thomas looked like a bearded skull set on a pile of rags. His eyes were socket-sized and fixed on me. "Oh my God, thank you, thank you, thank you," he said, and he was patting me, my legs and feet; at first I thought it was to make sure he wasn't hallucinating, that I was really there, but he was looking for water. When I handed him a bottle he drank so fast that it spilled over his lip and soaked his beard.

My back felt scraped where it had been pressing against the

wall. My knees would actually have been knocking, if I'd let them. It was surprisingly unquiet down there, something like the sound of being in a boiler room. My first order of business was to get my breathing under control; my chest felt like a pumping bellows. Pits, I realized, seem a lot deeper from their bottoms than from their tops. I could only see where I'd come from as a diffusing of my light. "What are we going to do?" Thomas said. "I'm hurt. I'm really hurt." The space we were in was slightly broader than the shaft we'd come down; it was about the size of a small elevator cab, with a dirt floor and rock walls, and he was sitting against a wall with one leg, his hurt leg, extended away from him, crying and talking to himself.

The next stretch of time divided itself into eras. Some of them lasted minutes, some of them lasted hours, but they were distinct periods, like the movements of a symphony. This one, immediately after I'd lowered myself into the pit, was the era of assessments and practicality. I knelt over his leg, as if I had the slightest idea what I was doing, and asked him what part hurt. His feet were bare, and he was still wearing the white terry-cloth robe from the hotel. His ankle, in my hands, felt thin enough to snap. I balanced the light on a little rock shelf next to us. It was his knee, it turned out; his kneecap was shiny and swollen, and when I touched it his whole body jumped. "OK," I said, "I don't think there's anything we can do about this right now."

Another characteristic of this era was that I was treating Thomas, and thinking of him, the way a fireman treats someone he finds gasping inside a house. I was hardly looking at his face. I wasn't saying a word about his disappearing from the hotel, or about his managing to have fallen down here. He was a trapped and damaged body and I was the person sent to save him.

I am, at best, an ordinarily strong person, and at that moment I was probably a good deal less than that, but Thomas was light enough that I was able, once I'd convinced him he was going to have to move, to pick him up like a barbell. My first set of attempts involved jumping, with him in my arms, and trying to lodge myself in the narrower part of the shaft, but I couldn't get nearly high enough. Then I tried getting a toehold on one of the tiny rock ledges a few feet off the ground, but I couldn't stay up for more than half a second, and even if I'd been able to, I wouldn't have been able to use my hands to climb any farther, because they were busy holding Thomas. He was moaning and babbling, the verbal equivalent of drooling. "Oh, it hurts, it hurts, it hurts, I'm sorry, I can't, I can't, I'm sorry." One of my most successful attempts was when I draped him over my shoulders like a mink scarf, then tried bracing myself against the walls with all four limbs spread out like Leonardo's *Vitruvian Man*. The basic problem was that the shaft, in a way I hadn't appreciated on the way down, was shaped more like a flask than like a test tube; we were stuck down in the fat part at the bottom.

I was actually managing to blot out my panic, or most of it, by keeping absolutely fixated on trying to get us out. Once I'd given up, for the moment, on jumping and climbing, I set about exploring the walls, in the hopes of finding another tunnel. For this I laid Thomas back down on the ground, his hurt knee in the air. "When was the last time you ate?" I said. "You need to eat." I gave him a cracker, which I ended up having to more or less stuff into his mouth, then ate most of one myself. It was around this point, I think, that I began to notice that the light from my flashlight, which had started out a fairly robust yellow white, was beginning to go ashen. Or maybe it had just shifted on its shelf. It had been running for only an hour or so, anyway, so I didn't think this was high on my list of things to worry about. I dropped to my knees and started feeling along the walls for places that might be made of something other than solid rock.

The most plausible patch turned out to be about the size and shape of an LP, right at ground level, on the wall where Thomas had been sitting when I'd first come in. There the rock, instead of feeling like the usual granite-ish slab, was almost crumbly. With my fingertips I managed to get a pretty good amount scraped off, and I was close to thinking I felt coolness, air, on the other side when I realized that what I was actually feeling was wetness; another surface of rock, just as solid as all the rest. I stayed there scraping at it for what must have been ten minutes, making no more progress than you would trying to scrape through stainless steel, and when I finally gave up it was the first moment in which I felt, unmistakably, the likelihood of death closing around me. It gave me a chill at a depth I didn't know was capable of feeling such things. Bone marrow, spinal fluid; there was no part of me that wasn't sending out distress signals.

There's a tendency, I think, to discount the suffering in fear; after the fact, once the tests have come back negative or the call's been returned, we think, *It wasn't as bad as all that.* We let our present relief retouch our past terror. I want to make sure I don't do that here; being down at the bottom of that pit, realizing I had no way of getting us out, was exactly as bad as all that.

I sat with my back against the wall and stared down at my legs, which were shaking freely. What the roar behind me sounded like more than anything, I realized, was a fire, a steadily approaching fire. My last act, I thought, might be murdering Thomas. He had his eyes gently closed and he was still muttering, almost soundlessly now. I kept looking up into the shaft, in case there might be a handhold, a shelf, a passageway I'd overlooked.

There was no question of the light's dimming, finally. The end of a flashlight is a terrible thing; it shrinks and closes in on itself like the last gulp of water down a bathtub drain. I shook it, hoping the batteries might knock some life into each other. I twisted it off and on, off and on, off and on. Finally, I threw the light, as hard as I'd thrown anything since the last time I'd played baseball, against the wall next to Thomas; it made a small and unsatisfying sound, before it rolled back and bumped against my foot. We were in the dark.

Q: Can you talk a little bit about guilt? That's something I struggle with a lot, going back over things I regret saying, people I regret hurting, all that sort of stuff, and I think it really gets in the way of my practice.

P: When feeling guilty, you are at the center of the story, yes? You are feeling, "Oh, I do so many things, I hurt so many people, me, me, me, me."

Q: So guilt is a kind of vanity, you're saying?

P: Guilt is story. Story is mind's way to say, "I understand, it is in my control," even if story is "Oh, I have no control, everything happening to me."

Q: So I should try to stop telling myself stories, whether they're good or bad?

P: Think of man holding a torch [*mimes picking up a torch*], and it is coming close to burning his fingers.

Man waves the torch, tries to press it against ground, runs looking for river, flame only getting closer, closer, closer. I am saying to him, "Just open your hand. Let it drop." No more burning. Yes?

———

There couldn't be more than a few hundred people alive who really know absolute darkness. Deep-sea divers, unlucky miners. People think of the bathroom in the middle of the night, or the road when your headlights go off. *Oh my God, it's pitch-black.* No, it isn't. Actual darkness isn't just not being able to make out shapes, or not being sure where the walls are. It's got more in common with blinding light than it does with ordinary basement darkness; it presses on you, it fills you up, it's all you can think about.

For a long time (I can't say how long; my sense of time, which I'd already thought was haywire, was now untethered completely) I just sat there in the dark and tried not to scream. Each breath I took, each movement, seemed to require as much effort and attention as a step on hot coals. Me breathing, Thomas muttering, the cave breathing; I couldn't tell one sound from another. My whole body was tensed, almost vibrating, in anticipation of some sort of explosion. There's an exquisiteness to the moment before a tantrum, a kind of delicious pinpoint pain. I'd forgotten. It's much more pleasant than the tantrum itself, anyway, which is all flailing and stumbling and shouting yourself hoarse. I'd forgotten that part too.

I did eventually scream; Thomas by then had fallen mostly silent. Again, I don't know for how long, and I can't even say what I shouted, except that it centered around the word *help,* but my throat was raw by the end of it. There was wall pounding too, in addition to the shouting. And kicking and shouldering and jumping and, at one especially hopeless point, biting: I scraped my teeth against the wall and spat a mixture of dirt and blood.

When Thomas and I were in middle school, first spending our afternoons together, we used to talk sometimes about what we'd do if we found out we had one week to live. Sometimes it would be a day, sometimes just an hour. Our answers were always along the lines of breaking into the houses of girls we knew and explaining that common sense dictated that they have sex with us. Running through school naked, telling all our teachers to go fuck themselves. We always seemed to imagine the news of our impending deaths as a liberation, as if our lives were dress shoes we couldn't wait to take off.

God, there's so little we understand, so little we're actually capable of imagining. How many times had I read about human remains found in caves? *A significant discovery, with the potential to reshape anthropologists' understanding of . . .* How had I not heard the screaming, the wheezing and weeping as the air ran out? Or what about Pompeii? I'd walked past those gray bodies as if they were mannequins, animals in a diorama, blithely waiting all these centuries to demonstrate everyday life in ancient Italy. No. Their deaths were horrible. I should have heard shrieking while I walked, sipping orange soda, behind my mom down those streets. I should have imagined skin melting like cheese.

I had a loose rock in one hand and I was pounding it, scraping it, against the ground. It didn't matter, I realized, whether my eyes were open or closed. If I learned I was about to die, it turned out that what I'd do is have the most staggeringly intense Technicolor panic attack of which a human body is capable. No sex. No running. No triumphant speeches.

Before the attack really took hold, though, or before it became so crippling that I wasn't capable of anything other than lying there and experiencing it, I did try talking to Thomas.

"What were you thinking?" I said. "What the fuck were you thinking?"

I didn't expect him to answer me, really. I had the impression by then that he was animate in some other way than I was, like a plant, or a reef. Instead, in a voice much more like the one he'd had in the hotel, he said, "This isn't what I wanted. This isn't what I meant to happen at all. I know it doesn't make any difference to you, but—"

"What did you think was going to happen?"

"I was supposed to . . . Once I got here and sat, something was supposed to change. I thought I would, maybe not leave my body, but I would understand that something had left, I would feel something, I would finally be free. But I fell, and I panicked. It was the worst I'd felt since . . . since I first met Guruji. I forgot why I was here. I got so thirsty I started to cry. And then you came, and I'm so grateful, I finally understand what you've done for me, but I wish you hadn't, because—"

"Because we're going to fucking die?"

"We are, yes, I am, I understand that now. And I understand that I needed to, that I always needed to die, for me to get where I'm going I couldn't live, and I just wish you didn't have to—"

If my consciousness had been a symphony, this next phase would have been the work of an experimental composer, someone shunned by the academy, someone whose pieces included things like musicians snapping their instruments over their knees and tearing up their sheet music. Bodily, I was now lying on my side, against the wall, every so often dipping my fingertip in the mouth of the water bottle to moisten my lips, but mentally, or anyway in the parts of the body that experience things invisibly, I was in hell. "Life flashing before my eyes" doesn't describe it, because flashes are brief, and because this wasn't my whole life, or even particularly important parts of it. It was more like someone had filled a row of buckets from the lake of my life, and now that person was dunking my head in them, one after another, until I nearly drowned.

One bucket:

I saw my mom sitting at the head of our kitchen table in Baltimore, eating soup from one of our chipped white bowls. The sky outside was silver; there was a sound somewhere of an airplane or an air conditioner. On the table in front of her, spread out under her bowl, was one of her health magazines. She had a big pale spoonful of broth and she was blowing on it in this way I would never have thought I remembered: the exact pattern of the wrinkles around her lips when she puckered, the precise little *shushing* noise. And for some reason the me in the memory was in agony; the sense was that I'd been told I had to wait for something, or that, as a punishment, I wasn't allowed to speak. There was a willful-ignoring quality in how she was blowing on the soup, I think, a kind of defiant unconcern. How old was I when this had happened? Six? Seven?

Another bucket:

I was in seventh grade, new to Dupont, and I was sitting in Principal Weaning's office, watching her pull the door shut. What had I done? I felt as if I were trying not to cry. One of the venetian blinds was bent. I could hear the phone ringing and then the secretary's voice out in the waiting room. There was a stringy half-dead plant on the windowsill. Now I remembered what I'd done: I'd lied that my real dad had been killed in a plane crash over the weekend in California. In homeroom, thinking it would be a joke, I'd leaned over to Scott Owens and whispered it, and then it had become too late: Justin Durand, Mrs. Nusk, shaky-handed sympathy hugs, a disastrous sense of being pinned in a trap. I was crying, wiping my nose with one of the thin and scraping tissues from the box on the desk, while Principal Weaning, her hands crossed in front of her, leaned toward me with a self-satisfied yellow smile and said, "Now, why did you lie, Adam? Why would you lie about something like that?"

On the floor of the cave, now, I was crying too, and shaking as if the ground beneath me had become electrified. Apparently drug addicts, in their first days of withdrawal, sweat out their substances; they writhe and scream and soak the sheets. "I hate you, Thomas," I heard myself saying. "I wish I'd never met you. I wish I'd never come."

"I'm sorry. I wish it had been someone else, I really do. I'm going to pray now, OK? I'm sorry, I need to, I'm sorry."

Another bucket, only it wasn't my life, it wasn't my memory:

It was the middle of the night and traffic lights were flashing and crickets were making a high hum, and I was standing alone on the curb of a familiar street. Everything had a kind of electron-microscope clarity: the glossiness of the asphalt, the ticking of the lights, the smell of the mulch, the reflections in the glass of the bus stop. I looked left, then stepped off the curb in a fluid hop. As I crossed the street I could feel, like a plunging thermometer, a car rolling out somewhere to my right. I couldn't turn my head but I knew it was there. The other car came more as a blaze of light than as an object; it wasn't there, and then it was.

At this point the memory, or whatever it was, branched in two, or maybe I branched in two. I was in my body and I was watching it. A piece of music with two parts.

The impact of a head against pavement is, when it happens, so ordinary; that's maybe the worst part about it. The laws that govern watermelons dropped from overpasses, pumpkins thrown from porches; they apply to our most precious possessions too. I can't say whether I jumped or screamed or what; I can only describe the feeling, which was pain, yes, the worst sort of ripping, brain-bursting pain, but also something much worse and much harder to explain. A kind of sinking into an icy ocean, maybe. The sort of falling you do in dreams but without the bolting awake: just down, down, down.

And then at some depth, streaming past, clearer than they'd been in actual life, were the Batras. Faces in a submarine window. The only way I can describe their expressions is: I knew I would rather be blind for the rest of my life than to have to look at them again. They were so clear I could see the tiny hairs in the pores of their cheeks. Words like *devastation, grief, horror, shock* are fingers pointing at an abyss; their faces were the abyss.

I must have screamed.

Somewhere far above me, or somewhere close but with many layers in between, I heard Thomas's voice; I felt his hands on my shoulders, heard him saying something; I could feel the words but couldn't understand them, they were like snowflakes or ash.

"Are we dead?" I said.

He didn't answer.

I was so, so tired, I wasn't sure if I'd actually managed to speak.

"I'm going to save you," Thomas said. "Like you saved me. I can't keep you from dying, but I can save you."

"OK."

"Can you hear me?"

"Yes."

"Say something if you can hear me."

"I am. I can hear you."

"Are you breathing?"

"Yes."

"If you're breathing, just feel it. Forget your name."

"I don't understand."

"You're breathing."

"Yes."

"You aren't dead."

"No."

"Can you hear me?"

"Yes."

"Move your hand if you can hear me."

I moved my hand.

"Something was switched on when you were born, and it's never been off, not for a second. Do you understand me?"

"No."

"It was there before you met me, before you met your mom. It's been running through the accident and the trip here and every conversation, every dream, there's been this thing; it never flinches, it never closes its eyes, not even now, it doesn't love or hate, it doesn't want or not want, nothing has ever happened to it. Do you understand?"

"No. Thomas, I'm so sorry. I'm tired. Please. I'm so sorry. I've made so many mistakes. I'm so, so tired."

"Squeeze my hand."

"I am."

"Just listen to me. You can fall back into it. It's always there. It doesn't care where we are. It doesn't care what we've done."

"I don't understand. Please."

"Just fall back. Fall."

"I can't."

But I could. Because I fell. And the thing in me I would have said was me—it was unplugged like a refrigerator. I hadn't known what silence was.

"Hello?" I said.

"Yes. You're talking."

"Thomas?"

I was still conscious, I'm pretty sure, but I was in rooms of my brain that I'd never been in. The best way to describe what I was experiencing then is to say that I'd been poured back into the lake. And that I understood, in the way you "understand" you have a body and a name, that it wasn't really my lake; I'd been, at most, a gallon or two; I was dissolved. And among the things I discovered, in this new state, was that it didn't matter anymore whether I was speaking out loud. I could talk to Thomas without opening my mouth. I could think at him.

Remember when we lay side by side on our backs on the sofa in your room and walked on the ceiling, stepped over doorways.

Yes.

Remember when we sat at the top of that hill in the sun eating a Kit Kat and said this was the happiest we'd ever be, that there was nothing else we'd ever need.

Yes.

Did you mean to stop the car?

I think so.

Did you think I would jump in the window?

I don't know.

Are we here as punishment?

I don't know.

Are we going to die?

Yes.

Do you forgive me?

Yes.

We were so young.

Yes.

The mistake was so small.

Yes.

The disaster was so big.

Yes.

My tears tasted salty and thin. I was rising, by that point, the sound was coming back into the world; I kept trying to open my eyes and realizing they were already open. My tongue was so dry it felt swollen. I could feel Thomas's shoulder against mine; he seemed to be propping me up; he was tipping water into my mouth. I had to struggle to keep myself from falling asleep.

"Now are we dead?"

"No."

I coughed and swallowed water.

The doors to the rooms where I'd been were still open, but I was back now in the ordinary, semi-ordinary, rooms of my brain; I didn't know whether an hour had passed or a week. I felt as if I were treading water in a pool that was exactly the same temperature as my body. I was both as heavy as the mountain we were trapped in and completely weightless. The roaring behind the walls was louder than it had ever been, and I was trying to say this to Thomas, trying to ask him whether he heard it too, but I couldn't remember what words to use, and it was too loud anyway.

Which may explain why the voices, when they finally sounded above us, seemed like such tiny things, negligible, raindrops against a window. I don't think I understood what was happening, that something was happening, until I looked up and saw light like a steel spike falling toward us; or maybe it wasn't until the rope, the wet rough knot of it, touched my arm. I just know that there was a lot of clattering and talking and then there was an era of people grabbing me, pulling me, as if I were a ball of dough, and then that I had my face buried in someone's chest, and I was clinging to a rope so hard that my eyes were flashing white. Afterward, once we were outside, they told me I kept insisting that we be careful with Thomas's leg, and that I kept asking him if he was OK, asking if he was with us, saying I was sorry, but I don't remember any of that.

What I do remember, the first thing that registers as an actual memory, rather than as a kind of mental oil rainbow, is walking, with my arm slung over Ranjiv's shoulder, up out of the cave and realizing, once the brightness had begun to resolve itself, that it was pouring rain. Standing there on a ledge just outside the mouth of the cave, like the discoverer of a new continent, dripping, squinting, shaking, I felt newborn; I felt like Frankenstein's monster, stitched together from spare parts.

Ranjiv had been having doubts all the way back to Akki's village, it turned out. He'd almost turned around a dozen times before he'd finally decided what he was going to do.

He'd told Akki, who'd bought rope and lights and borrowed a little Soviet-era ATV sort of thing from a nearby village. It had, according to the clocks aboveground, been just over thirty-six hours since I'd gone in, and almost twice that long for Thomas.

But I didn't know any of that yet. I just knew that I somehow wasn't dead. And that the rain sounded like a thousand drumrolls. It might have been the contrast to the sensory deprivation of being underground, but I think it really was the kind of rainstorm you only experience two or three times in your life, the kind of rain during which you think, *I guess the world's just going to wash away.* There wasn't, by the time they'd crammed us into the back of the ATV and covered us with a tarp, a thread of my clothing, including my shoes, that wasn't soaked. I was wetter than if I'd jumped into a swimming pool. I heard a voice I didn't recognize that must have been the car-owning neighbor's. We had a four-hour drive ahead of us and every muscle in my body hurt. Someone had put a horsehair blanket under my head, and that was soaked too. I kept calling out to Thomas, thinking he might have fallen out of the car on one of the bumps, and he kept being just a few inches away, wedged and shivering next to me. The only food Akki and the monks had brought with them were crackers that tasted like pepper. The rain was so loud that we couldn't have talked even if we'd tried. It seemed inconceivable that we'd ever get there; it seemed possible at any moment that we'd flip onto our side and be washed away.

But the thought that kept floating to the top of my mind like an ice cube in a glass, even as I shivered and shook and tried to bite the cracker someone held against my lips, was: What a narrow range of weathers we have in mind when we describe a day as beautiful! Water is falling, in gouts and cups and gushes, from the sky, onto us, who can feel and hear and smell and taste it. What a lock! What a key! Breathable air, spread out in every direction. Trees and dirt and rocks for us to look at, teeth with which to chew our food. This is most of what I was thinking, if you can call it thinking, all the way back to Akki's front door, where it was nighttime, and where Shima greeted us with dry blankets and scalding tea. This, or something like this, is even what I was thinking when they finally changed me into dry pajamas and eased Thomas and me into side-by-side beds, and I fell into a sleep that was almost a hibernation. Akki's disappointment, the questions I couldn't even try to answer, a look at the shaking, bruised wrecks of our bodies, came much later.

Before I fell asleep, though, or before I lost touch completely with what was happening, I said to Thomas, or thought to Thomas, "Are we still in the cave?"

"No."

"So we lived?"

"I think so, yes."

What I felt, when I finally believed it, wasn't entirely relief. Or if it was, it was a different sort of relief from any I'd ever felt before. Because I remembered now what I'd been thinking when we were being saved, when Ranjiv was reaching down and lifting me up like a sack of feathers. It was the strangest thing; it felt, even as I knew that this meant life, and food, and light, like being handed the wrong jacket at a party. I'd tried to say something. There had been a misunderstanding. We didn't need rescuing at all.

· *Four* ·

From: \<Adam Sanecki>
To: \<Thomas Pell>
Date: Thu, Aug 20, 2009 at 3:28 PM
Subject: (no subject)

Hey. I feel like an astronaut asking to get together for coffee after a mission. I just wanted to see how you're holding up. I'm weird but all right—panicky, elated, weepy,
etc. Give me a call or write sometime. I've got lots of time
to talk and very few people to talk to.

From: <Adam Sanecki>
To: <Thomas Pell>
Date: Wed, Sep 9, 2009 at 5:34 PM
Subject: (no subject)

Hey. I was just writing to pester you about my last email when your parents called.

Your mom says you agreed to try the hospital. I think (a) you're doing the right thing, and (b) it probably won't feel like the right thing at first. So (not that you're looking for my advice on this) bear with it.

Things with me have been more normal the past couple of weeks. At first I was spending too much time walking around the streets by my apartment, staring at people, sitting by the Barnes & Noble fountain, studying the brickwork. I thought maybe I'd inhaled poison in the cave, that I might end up the happy, slow-talking homeless person of Bethesda.

I've been writing back and forth with your parents a little (I hope that's OK). They asked me to come over for dinner, but I've been putting them off. Pretty sure they just want to thank me and hear more about India, etc., but I'm worried I'd blurt out the whole story of the Batras. Have you thought about telling them? I'm not sure what would come of it (I'm not sure about anything), but part of me thinks it would be good for everybody.

Tell me how you're doing once you're settled in.

From: <Adam Sanecki>
To: <Thomas Pell>
Date: Wed, Nov 4, 2009 at 9:58 PM
Subject: (no subject)

Hey. You know how you can tell when someone's on the other end of the phone, even if they don't talk? Well, I'm OK with you not responding to my emails. Your mom says your computer use is limited, and I can tell (I think) that you're reading them.

I got a note from your dad yesterday, who says you're looking good. I'm going to call the hospital as soon as I send this to find out about visiting hours, etc.

Not much doing with me. I got that apartment in Foggy Bottom. I've been trying to learn how to cook—so far mostly roast chicken and omelets, for some reason. My mom's been sending me three recipes a day from the Food Network (*Carving the tops of the scallions might seem like a lot of work, but your guests will love you for it!*).

Hope you're good. Carve a scallion.

From: \<Adam Sanecki\>
To: \<Thomas Pell\>
Date: Wed, Dec 2, 2009 at 8:09 PM
Subject: (no subject)

Hey. Kind of a weird question. I told you about that girl I was dating, Sonia—things have gotten semiserious. She's in her residency at GW, very smart, funny, etc. I've said "I love you" to an embarrassing number of girlfriends, but this is the first time I can picture meaning something by it other than "Oh my God, please don't break up with me!" Anyway, I was thinking I might want to tell her about Mira. Would very much appreciate your thoughts.

What else. I'm still listening to those Guruji-lite audiobooks. I hide them in the glove compartment whenever someone other than Sonia's going to be in the car. Still not used to hearing these magnetic poetry sentences coming out of my speakers. *We only truly suffer when we resist what is. Our capacity to love others is in perfect proportion to our capacity to love ourselves.* Better than whatever I was living by before, though. (*If something bad might happen, think about it. Never let an email arrive without witnessing its appearance.*)

Hope you're good. Detonate a gut-bomb for me.

From: <Adam Sanecki>
To: <Thomas Pell>
Date: Sat, Jan 30, 2010 at 8:41 PM
Subject: (no subject)

Hey. Good to see you last week. You do look good (probably not something we've ever said to each other). Didn't
know how to tell you in person, but I told Sonia about Mira.
She was really good about it. I had to stop halfway through
because I thought I'd burst a blood vessel. She's the first
person I've ever told, it occurred to me. We were driving
somewhere the other day and she said, "Wait, so is this why
we never go on Connecticut?" I honestly hadn't realized.

She said she thought I should call the other driver. We got
into a fight about it; I said there was no point, she said it
was cruel, I said he'd probably moved by now, etc., etc. I'd
pretty much decided not to, but then I found myself searching the *Post* archives for Charles Lowe and before Sonia
came home the other night I was dialing a 202 number. I
know I should have told you about it before I did it, but I

didn't want to wait. The conversation was short, like maybe five minutes. He didn't believe who I was at first. He refused to see me. He sounded like someone who'd grown up in New York or New Jersey, someone with a scary dog.

"You and your friend wrecked my fucking life, you know."

"I don't know what to say. I'm sorry."

"I should wreck yours too. I could do it with one phone call."

"I understand. I'm sorry."

He went away for long enough that I thought he might be making his one life-wrecking phone call, but then he came back and he sounded like he was drinking something. "You know, that girl, she doesn't belong on my conscience."

"No."

"That family, they were good to me, they believed me. No charges, nothing like that."

"I know."

Before he hung up, he said something so kind I almost dropped the phone. "You guys were fucking kids. Just fucking kids."

And that was it.

So he's not going to call the police or kill us or anything. And I think talking to him did something good for me. I read somewhere there are two kinds of guilt: the sweaty, frantic, four-in-the-morning kind, where you almost wish you'd get caught, and a quieter, sadder kind, where it feels like you're sitting on a rainy beach, looking out at the water. I feel like calling him might have pushed me from the first kind to the second. (I should probably go easy on the audiobooks, it occurs to me.)

From: <Adam Sanecki>

To: <Thomas Pell>

Date: Mon, Mar 1, 2010 at 6:14 PM

Subject: (no subject)

Hey. I'm just back from visiting you. I came there meaning to tell you something, and I managed to spend the whole hour not doing it. Much easier to talk about Sonia and law school applications, it turns out. Maybe you got Raymond's note too (I'm not sure if he'd have your email, actually) but Sri Prabhakara is dead. He died last week. He was ninety or so, and he had a heart attack in his sleep. There's a service for him at the center in a couple of weeks. I couldn't think of how to say it, but I should have told you. I'm sorry.

From: <Adam Sanecki>
To: <Thomas Pell>
Date: Mon, Mar 29, 2010 at 9:14 PM
Subject: (no subject)

Hey. Reassure me the phone line isn't dead, OK? I can't
tell if it's me being paranoid or an actual change (me
being paranoid's usually a pretty good bet), but I've been
getting a weird feeling. Things are good/normal with me.

From: <Richard Pell>

To: <Adam Sanecki>

Date: Sat, Apr 24, 2010 at 8:44 PM

Subject: re: greetings

Adam—

I hope this finds you well. Your mother tells us you've got a serious girlfriend—this is, I know, just the kind of thing twentysomethings most like for their friends' parents to discuss in the lobbies of movie theaters. Anyway, bring her by the house sometime and we promise to feed you well and embarrass you minimally.

Some fretful Thomas news—he's still in the hospital, but lately threatening to check himself out (Kafka ghostwrote the laws regarding committing an adult against his will, I'm fairly sure). Also—and please don't repeat this to him, since he seems to have taken his correspondence with you as one of his refuges from all the medico-parental aspects of his life—his doctor told us this morning that he seems not to be taking his pills. Unsure how new a development this is, but alarm bells are jangling in Sally and me. He's had the usual litany of complaints with the pills— fuzzy-headedness, bloatedness, etc.—but they were seeming to do the job, taking the more worrisome items off his mental menu. And lately those items have been creeping back, so we'd already been concerned: lots of ordinary words used in unordinary ways—*becoming, seeing, falling, opening*. Mainly it's been a look, though, which I'm sure you became acquainted with in India—a strong impression of having his thoughts on matters over the horizon, which is, the doctors tell us, precisely the wrong place for them to be.

We've already imposed on you more than anyone could reasonably—or unreasonably—ask, but I wonder if you'd be willing to keep writing to him, visiting him, etc., and if you could—if you think it's warranted—reassure us about whether there's been a change, whether the story seems to you about to tip back into crisis. We've come to trust your vision in all this much more than our own, and to a certain extent even more than the doctors'. I think there's a sport in making authority figures wring their hands, and Thomas has become all too skilled at it. My sense is that there's less nonsense between the two of you, and that you might be able to tell us whether this is the sort of thing that could be cleared up with some family sessions and pharmacological tweaks, or if it's something, again, entirely other.

Fretfully,

Richard

From: <Adam Sanecki>
To: <Thomas Pell>
Date: Wed, May 5, 2010 at 5:07 PM
Subject: (no subject)

Hey. You probably already know this but I tried visiting you yesterday. The desk person told me you or your doctors had put in a no-visitors note, which is totally fine, of course, but I just wanted to make sure you're all right. Things are good with me. It's Sonia's birthday, so about to spend a painful amount of money on dinner. Let me know how you're doing.

Adam,

I'm grateful for your emails, for your visits, I understand
the feeling of duty, I don't dismiss it, I only hope you
realize the things my parents tell you are not the actual
matters, they talk to doctors, gorge on gossip, the only
course is to nod and murmur and keep things simple, life
as a series of chores, a list to be dispatched, one second
after another. I'm not complaining, not entirely complaining, their concern is misguided but not malicious, I was
going to go home, but now I won't, the being watched is
too much, and the simplicity here does me good, it keeps
me settled, I don't feel fears, the fears I feel are not so
full of hidden edges, the last drops of medicine will be
out of me soon. What I want to tell you, the only thing I
want to tell you, is not for my parents, is not to reassure

you, I won't be living an ordinary life, renting an apartment, tiptoeing around what happened in India, riding the
Metro, telling people all is well. We did a terrible thing, I
won't say accident, we owe it to her not to waste it. What
I want to say is that for the first twenty-seven years of
our lives we were asleep, we were having bad dreams.
Sleep is a vault, we dream inside it, weaving what sense
we can from the scratches, the scrapes that make it to us
from outside. I hope, I trust, your dreams are better now.
I know you're happy, I read your letters, I've seen your
eyes, your trimmed nails, your shirts that someone else
picked out. What you felt in the cave, I held your limbs
as they twitched, was the moment in a dream when the
noise outside becomes too loud, your eyelids flutter, your
machinery falters, you grunt but don't speak, and then
you slip back into the dream but at another angle. I did
die in the cave, I know that now, I was empty after that,
the person you saw was not the person you knew, my
parents, my doctors, even, I'm sorry, you, Adam, you've
been calling into a tunnel and having conversations with
the echoes. I knew it when Guruji died, you didn't have
to tell me, I felt the change, I'd been waiting and it came,
and now I'm learning, relearning, what I have to do, but
you don't have to worry, you can keep living, keep writing,
keep sitting on your rainy beach and saying "gut-bomb"
and feeling more or less happy, I wouldn't blame you for
it. But I just want to tell you, if you do change your mind,
if questions catch hold of you, if you can bring yourself,
after everything, to trust me, that your quietest doubts are
right, and that what seems, on sleepless nights, not to
be a life in fact is not. I want to say there's more, there's
always more, for you to do: it will feel like waking up.

Acknowledgments

Thanks to Doug Stewart, Jennifer Jackson, Bryan, Nishant, Sam, Heidi, and my parents.

About the Author

Ben Dolnick lives in Brooklyn with his wife. He is the author of the novels *You Know Who You Are* and *Zoology,* and his work has appeared in *The New York Times* and on NPR.

A Note on the Type

The text of this book was set in Garamond No. 3. It is not a true copy of any of the designs of Claude Garamond (ca. 1480–1561) but an adaptation of his types, which set the European standard for two centuries. It probably owes as much to the designs of Jean Jannon, a Protestant printer working in Sedan in the early seventeenth century, who had worked with Garamond's romans earlier, in Paris, but who was denied their use because of Catholic censorship. Jannon's matrices came into the possession of the Imprimerie nationale, where they were thought to be by Garamond himself and were so described when the Imprimerie revived the type in 1900. This particular version is based on an adaptation by Morris Fuller Benton.

Typeset by Scribe, Philadelphia, Pennsylvania
Printed and bound by Berryville Graphics,
Berryville, Virginia